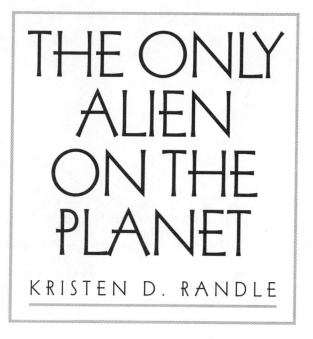

THE ONLY ALIEN ON THE PLANET

KRISTEN D. RANDLE

SCHOLASTIC
HARDCOVER

Scholastic Inc.
New York

Library of Congress Cataloging-in-Publication Data
Randle, Kristen D.
The Only Alien on the Planet / Kristen D. Randle.
p.   cm.
Summary: After moving to the East Coast, Ginny enters her senior
year of high school and uncovers the secret behind a new friend's
refusal to speak.
ISBN 0-590-46309-8
[1. Moving, Household — Fiction. 2. Friendship — Fiction.
3. Mutism, Elective — Fiction. 4. High schools — Fiction.
5. Schools — Fiction.] I. Title.
PZ7.R158501   1994
[Fic] — dc20   93-34594
                                                        CIP
                                                        AC

12 11 10 9 8 7 6 5 4 3 2 1   5 6 7 8 9/9 0/0

Printed in the U.S.A.   37

First Scholastic printing, March 1995

For
Meridee and Rebecca
who are willing

For
Bebee
who won't let you quit

and for
Tonya
who, it seems,
is also given to visions.

THE ONLY ALIEN ON THE PLANET

CHAPTER ONE

The first time I ever saw Smitty Tibbs, I was having one of the worst days of my life. Truth — up till then, I'd been a happy person — happy, cheerful, confident, easygoing, reasonably popular even. Well-adjusted, in other words. Everything in my life had always been so balanced, so friendly, so *dependable*.

And then my brother Paul — probably my best friend in the world, up and left for college. It was the biggest shock I'd ever had. *"This should not be a big surprise for you,"* he'd said to me. And he was right. It's just, I wasn't ready for it, somehow, and the reality ended up hitting me in the face like a bucket of ice water. I couldn't figure out how Paul had all of a sudden gotten so old. When I said that very thing to my mother a couple of months ago, she pointed out that I just happened to be starting *my* last year of high school, talk about people growing up.

I wish she'd said anything but that.

We've always had this tight little family: my three brothers, me, and our two parents. My mom'd had us kids in five and a half years' worth of marathon pregnancy. ("I always wanted you guys to be close," she says now. "Just don't ask me to do it again.") So living in our house had been a little like being raised in some kind of crazy boys' dorm.

We'd always lived in the same house, in a middle-sized town where everybody who counted knew our names, in the West where there are always great sunsets and never any winter, and all of my friends whom I'd known since kindergarten. Everything well-ordered, solid and wholesome — constant as the earth under your feet. *"Too darned comfy,"* Paul would say.

It never even crossed my mind that things could ever change; I just figured we'd go on that way forever — always, always, always, as natural as breathing. Stupid kid that I was, I thought it just Life.

"But I've gotta go," Paul had said. *"The only way to get things to stand still is for us all to die at the same time. And I don't think we're all going to be into that."* So, he paid his tuition, packed up — it was like the ground fell out from under me, and I didn't know where I was anymore. Actually, I was right about that; I'd been living in a beautiful dream that was coming to an awful, sickening end.

A month and a half before Paul actually departed for the Mysterious Beyond, my dad comes out with this announcement: "The good old ancestral air is going a little stale. I think, dear family, we need a little stirring up."

Stirring up.

And what, exactly, did he mean by that? I'll tell you what he meant: He intended to sell our good old house and move us thousands of miles *east*.

"I promise you *Winter* . . ." he says, like he's performing some kind of great magic, ". . . *Autumn,*

2

White *Christmases*. A House with a Fireplace. New *Faces*. New *Norms*. Fresh Blood. My children — this may very well be our *Great Adventure*."

"What about the stuff we've already got?" I pointed out. "What about *familiar* faces? What about *old* norms?" But the boys bought it. The boys would have bought snake oil, too. My mother, on the other hand, is a stable, reasonable kind of person; she likes money in the bank and old friends and things of familial historical significance. I kept waiting for her to *do* something, to tell Dad this was the stupidest idea he'd ever had.

But *no*. She just sat there, smiling, while he stuck signs in our yard and signed papers and made us go through all the stuff in the attic.

And suddenly, there I was, Ginny Christianson, displaced person, sitting at a marked-up desk a thousand miles from home, in the middle of a school filled with hundreds, maybe thousands, of people who didn't even know they didn't know me.

"*A new life*," Paul had said to me. "*Built on the beautiful model of the old one. Take hold, old Gin. Attack it the way you would a wild windmill.*"

Nobody was talking to me. Nobody needed me. Nobody even knew I was there.

I was totally alone for the first time in my life.

And I really hated the way it felt.

I decided then and there — no Great Adventure is worth this kind of pain. No new life is worth demoting the old one to Beautiful Model. No Great Adventure will ever be worth the price. I swore to myself, feeling a lot like Scarlet O'Hara, *I'll never go wandering again*. Give me a safe, warm hearthside and comfortable, old furniture; give me familiar,

3

beloved faces — definitely, I am a fan of the Known and Constant Universe.

In a desperate bid for sanity, I told myself, *This is the first day of school for all these people; everybody's got to be a little off balance.* I could hear Paul telling me, *"Never, never make the mistake of thinking you're the only alien on the planet."*

But that's exactly the way I did feel — different desks, different schedule, halls and halls and halls that all looked the same to me. Everybody else knew their way around. I might as well have been a million light years from home.

And lost.

Then, all of a sudden, this girl across the aisle — one of those very cute, totally secure-looking people; somebody like I might have been, myself, once, in another life — smiled at me. "I don't know your face," she said to me. "You a transfer? Or did you just move in?"

"Just moved in," I said, hoping my mouth didn't look as rubbery and stupid as it felt. It was like I was hearing my own voice from the outside, and I didn't sound natural.

"I hate being new," she said, commiserating. "You just feel so — off-register, you know what I mean?"

The image was lost on me, but I was pretty sure I knew what she meant, so I smiled, and she smiled, and things began to seem not so utterly desolate.

"I'm Hally," she told me.

"My name's Ginny," I answered, still sounding like a total nebbish.

But Hally didn't seem to notice. She was too busy asking me stuff — where I was from and what I liked to do. She finally hauled out her schedule, and made me show her mine. As it happened, they turned out to match almost exactly.

She glanced over my shoulder and started to grin. "Not a bad start," she whispered to me. "Scott Holyoak's over there giving you the eye."

"Is that good?" I whispered back.

"Ain't bad," she laughed. "Yep. He's interested, all right."

So, of course, I glanced back over my shoulder, and that was the first time I saw Smitty Tibbs.

Just then, the bell rang and the teacher came through the door. I never got the pleasure of embarrassing Scott Holyoak. I never even saw him. It was the boy in the far corner of the front row that caught me by the eyes and made me forget just about everything else in the world. This unearthly, beautiful boy.

"Okay, people," the teacher was saying, and I remembered where I was. I glanced at Hally apologetically, suspecting I'd just made a total fool of myself. She was watching me, the smile gone. She narrowed her eyes slightly and gave her head this ghost of a shake. It was not an unfriendly look. More like a concerned warning. The whole thing was very disconcerting.

The noise in the room had now settled to a soft rustle. Hally smiled at me once more, and gave me this little shrug.

The teacher had just finished writing MS. STERN on the blackboard and she turned to face us, all hard, bright business — obviously your very dedicated kind of woman. With something like a collective spiritual sigh, we all slid back in our seats and let her start the year.

I really tried to listen, but once you've heard the *This is English and You're Going to Take it Seriously* spiel, it's hard to get excited for the reruns. My mind began to wander, and so did my eyes — back to that far corner of the front row. Back to the most beautiful human being I'd ever seen.

The interesting thing about it was that, the more I looked at him, the less I understood what I was seeing. At second glance, he really wasn't physically all that remarkable — medium-sized body, medium-length, light-brown curls — squeaky clean but not especially groomed. (I always check out a person's hair right off; I think you can tell a lot about somebody, looking at the way they have their hair. All this hair said to me was "neat and clean and not particularly concerned.") His clothes were okay — on the conservative side, but with a little bit of style.

It was something in his face that got to you; he had a sort of angelic air, clear and distant and pure, like he'd never had a bad thought in his life. And strange — there was something really strange about him.

The room had gotten very quiet.

"I'll make sure she picks one up," Hally was saying.

I came to myself and realized that everybody was watching me. My cheeks started getting hot, and I caught this *You have only minutes to live* look from the teacher. Great way to start out. *This girl's an idiot.* Right then, I was sure I was doomed — but then Hally gave me this little wink. It was kind of her. And that single, insignificant, kind act suddenly shone like a tiny sun in the dark void that had been looming in my future. All of a sudden, I knew Hally was going to be my friend. It was like finding my center of gravity.

"I'd forgotten how pretty he is till I saw your face this morning," Hally was saying as she dug for a book in the bottom of her locker. "I guess I should have warned you, but I really didn't even think of it."

"Is there — " I asked, trying to read her attitude, " — something wrong with him?"

"Some people think he's autistic," she said, pulling the book out and shoving everything else back in. She stood up, trying to balance all the books she had stacked up on her notebook. "Myself, I wouldn't know." She slammed her locker shut. "Mr. Leviaton — I think you've got him — fifth period, world history. Yeah, you do, see? Smitty's kind of a pet of his. He says no way it's autism." She gave the lock an absent spin.

"Smitty."

"Smitty Tibbs. Sounds like a name you'd give a puppy or something, doesn't it? Come on." She started off down the hall. "Anyway," she went on, "*something's* seriously wrong with him."

I considered that, dodging a couple of freshmen who were chasing each other down the middle of the hall. "Like, what is it he does that's weird?"

"Smitty Tibbs has never said a word to anybody." Hally waved at a kid down the hall. There must have been about fifty people who'd said "hi" to her on our way to second period. "And he never smiles, and he never frowns, and he never cries. He's always been that way. If you talk to him, he doesn't react — it's like he doesn't hear you. It's really like he's not aware there's anybody else in the universe."

She stopped and readjusted the books.

"So what's he doing here in this school?" I asked. "Is it some kind of social integration program or something?"

She laughed. "That's a better question than you know. The really weird thing is, he's totally brilliant. Top honor roll, every semester. There's this story around that Mr. Leviaton secretly had Smitty sit down and make up an exam for him — questions, answer key, the whole thing — and then Mrs. Fliecher, the principal, gave the test to the whole faculty in faculty meeting one day, without telling them what it was. They hated it."

"And that really happened?" I asked, doubting it.

She shrugged and pointed. "Down those stairs. No, to the left. The thing is, it *could* be true. So I don't know what he's doing in this school. He should probably be at MIT or Johns Hopkins or something."

"This is weird," I said.

"Tell me about it. He's definitely one of the Great Mysteries in our lives."

I shook my head, thinking it over. "I'm amazed he's made it this far alive. You guys must be very civilized. It's sad, but he probably wouldn't have lasted five minutes in my old school."

"Yeah, well," she said. "He really had it hard for a while here, early on." She jumped. "Knock it off, Jesperson." She slapped at somebody behind us. "One day in the first grade" — she shifted her notebook — "a whole bunch of kids had knocked him down on the playground. It was really awful — they were kicking him, and it was just — " She clenched her teeth. "I was really furious." Then she grinned fiercely. "But along came Caulder Pretiger, like an avenging angel out of heaven, and within about thirty seconds, those kids were scattered like spit in the wind. It was wonderful. Nobody messed with Smitty after that because they were all too scared of Caulder." Her eyes were flashing.

Then she shrugged, shifting gears. "They probably wouldn't want to try anything with him these days — he's not exactly your defenseless little wimp anymore. The worst they do now is make stupid jokes. And they call him 'The Alien' sometimes, which is not totally inaccurate considering he definitely *is* from another planet. It's just kind of ironic they'd call *him* that, like they're all so normal, themselves."

She sighed. "Actually, I don't think anybody really notices him that much anymore. I mean, he looks normal enough, doesn't he? And you get used to people after a while. And I don't know," she grinned. "Maybe they're all still scared of Caulder."

She stopped in front of a classroom door. "Now you know everything I know." She pulled the door open. "Advanced trig," she announced, looking anything but excited. "Welcome to the math class from hell —"

That afternoon, the Christiansons had a little family council. We sat on scavenged stools under the one overhead light in the new living room, surrounded by piles of boxes and mounds of books

9

and other stuff we hadn't organized yet, feeling like intruders in that empty, echoing house. There, our folks told us about the beautiful old Victorian building they'd found downtown, the absolutely perfect new home for Christianson Graphic Design.

"The only thing is," my mother said, "it's going to take a lot of work, getting that place in working order. A *lot* of work. And it's not like we've got a lot of money lying around just now" — here, she sent my father a pointed look — "so your dad and I are going to have to be doing a lot of the work ourselves. Wiring and painting and stuff." Then she looked at Dad like she wasn't real convinced about the thing she meant to say next.

"And the point of all this?" James prompted.

"The point is," my father responded, "you guys are going to have to be pretty much on your own for the next few weeks."

"Maybe this isn't such a good idea," Mom said to him.

Dad looked at us. "Understand, this means we're going to be down there all day every day — and probably into the night, trying to get this thing going before we all starve. . . ."

"Are you suggesting that this is going to be a problem?" Charlie asked.

Mom looked at him like he'd just proven her point. "You're going to be cooking for yourselves," she said, ticking things off on her fingers, "doing the laundry, the unpacking, the housekeeping, fielding *any* problems that come up — and it means that you're going to have to get along, which may be harder than you think, considering the circumstances. And you're going to have to be responsible. Nobody's going to be here to pull you out of trouble, or yell at you for not doing your homework. Getting the picture?"

"I do all my own laundry anyway," James sniffed. Mom gave him one of her *yeah, sure* looks.

"You taught us all about nutrition, Mom, remember," Charlie said, consolingly. "It's not like we're going to die of rickets or something."

"Yeah, well — one of the responsible adults in this house will get a lunch made for you people every morning before we leave for downtown. That'll be one halfway intelligent meal a day, anyway. And, you *will* be able to call us there, once we have the phones in. But till then, you're going to be pretty much orphans."

Wonderful. Another great stride for my sense of inner peace and security.

"Just remember," my father said, "the sooner we get this building done, the sooner we'll be in business. The sooner we're in business, the sooner you can start asking us for money."

"We *had* a business back home," I said. A little flicker of anger had come up from some place way down under, a place that should have been shut up tighter than it evidently was.

My mother looked at me. "That's true," she said. "But we're here now. And we want to make this work." She was still looking at me. "On every possible level. Things are a little different right now, I know. But you've got to keep in mind — nothing important has changed."

So Paul not living with us anymore wasn't important.

"So, you guys going to support us in this?" Dad asked. "Can we depend on you?"

My mom was studying us. Studying me. "Is this a realistic expectation?"

James rolled his eyes. Charlie grinned.

"Of course," I lied, not looking at anybody in particular.

"Fine," she said. "James, you're in charge of laundry, since you're such an expert. Charlie, the kitchen. Ginny, you're in charge of making sure Charlie gets off that piano often enough to eat and sleep, okay? Okay? All right. I'm really proud of you guys. In advance. Thank you for being willing."

I hate being thanked for stuff I definitely cannot take credit for.

"Now, get out of here," Dad said. "Your mom and I have to discuss finances."

The man knew how to clear a room; my parents' financial "discussions" were the stuff of legend. Great friends as they were, money had a way of heating the both of them up, and you never wanted to get caught in that cross fire.

So, we found ourselves sort of ganged together on the front stoop, dismally surveying the yard. We didn't have a whole lot of options. Things could have been worse; it was an absolutely gorgeous day, the lawn was nice, and the trees were of a respectable size. "Baseball," Charlie said, brightening, and disappeared back into the house. He emerged a few moments later, triumphant, but "Lucky," he informed us, "to have escaped with my life."

"You wanna play?" Charlie asked me. "Or you

12

want to read?" He dangled a book in front of me, most enticingly.

"What a nice boy you are," I said, snagging the book. James and Charlie jumped down onto the lawn and started tossing the baseball back and forth, pausing every so often to trade cheerful insults. I took the book over to the side and stretched out on the grass under one of the trees. I just lay there for a moment, the sun warm on my legs, and the grass cool under my arms. I sighed. It felt cleansing.

"Science fiction?" somebody asked.

I blinked into the sunlight, and saw this boy leaning lazily over the side fence. I looked down at the cover of my book. "Yep," I said.

He straightened up. "I thought you'd be more into the classics." He smiled at me.

"Really," I said. "And what would make you think that?"

"Rumor," he said. "My mother told me you were a very serious family."

"And how would your mother know?"

"Your mother told her."

"Ahh," I said, and I put the book down.

"My name is Caulder," he said. "We have some classes together."

"I'm Ginny," I said, and I stood up.

"May I come and sit?" he asked.

I could hear the faint voices of my parents, discussing at each other.

"Sure," I said, and I sat back down on the grass. He came over the fence.

"Caulder is your last name?" I asked.

"No," he said, standing there, squinting at the boys. "It's a family name. My whole name is Caulder McKay Pretiger." He grinned down at me. "My family has a terrific sense of humor." He sat. He was a kind of normal-looking boy, with a wide mouth that seemed used to smiling and tousled brown hair that didn't say a thing about vanity. His eyes gave everything important away — there was mischief in them.

"I heard something about you today," I said, remembering, suddenly. "What was it? Something Hally told me."

"Hally," he said, and he seemed a little surprised.

"I know what it was. It was about that guy in my homeroom — "

"Smitty," he supplied, no question.

Now, I guess *I* looked surprised.

"It's my claim to fame," he shrugged. I couldn't read his tone, but I imagined he sounded a little bored, maybe even a little disappointed. So, I changed the subject.

"How long have you lived here?"

"All my life," he said. "And Smitty lives just on the other side."

"He lives over there?" I asked, staring. There was an immaculate, gray Cape Cod house on the far side of Pretiger's neat white picket fences. A large man in gray coveralls was standing in the driveway by the back of the house, wiping his hands on an oily rag.

"Smitty has a driver's license," Caulder said, almost dreamily. He had his eyes closed, holding his face up to the sun. My eyes popped open. "They'd let somebody like that *drive?*"

Caulder looked at me and smiled. "Not really. So, how did your first day turn out?"

I shrugged. "Hally was about the only person who really talked to me," I said. "I'm her friend for life."

"Everybody likes Hally," he said.

"She seemed to know everybody in the world." To put it mildly.

"Last year, she was captain of the forensics squad," he said. "This year, she's editor of the senior class literary magazine. She's kind of your Woman of the People. The amazing thing is, she's genuine."

I was kind of amazed that she'd noticed me at all. "Hally told me about the way you kind of watch over what's-his-name. 'Like a guardian angel,' I think she said."

He laughed. He had a healthy laugh.

"Well, that's what she said. She said you once fought off a nasty mob of crazed first-graders."

The laugh settled into a comfortable chuckle. "Yeah, well — she'd pretty much pounded them all herself before I ever got there."

"Oh, yeah?" I asked.

"Oh, yeah. Hally's a little hellion. If the same thing happened tomorrow, you can bet your life, she'd be right in the middle of it all over again, kicking the stuffing out of Tommy Quince."

"Really," I said, liking her better every minute.

"Yeah," he said, grinning. "Don't get on her bad side."

"Like, don't commit any social injustices while she's looking?"

"You got it."

I lay back in the grass with my hands behind

my head and my feet crossed, feeling good. "She said people think what's-his-name — Timmy? Scotty? She said they think he's autistic or something."

"Smitty. He's not." Caulder tossed the blade of grass away. "I've also heard people say he's an idiot savant," he said. "But that's not true either."

"So, what's true?" I asked him.

He leaned back in the grass and cocked his head to one side. "I really don't know," he said, finally — carefully.

The baseball came dropping down through the branches, not three feet from where we were sitting.

"Sorry," Charlie panted, grabbed the ball, and was gone.

"He could talk if he wanted to," Caulder said. "Smitty, I mean."

I just looked at him.

"I've always had a feeling," Caulder said.

"So, you're telling me, for seventeen years, he just hasn't felt like it."

"Look," he said. "His mother doesn't dress him. He dresses himself; he chooses his own clothes, same way you and I do. I mean, when you look at him, isn't it obvious he cares how he looks? He makes choices all the time — functional choices. His grades are perfect. You know what his SAT scores were? You know how close you can get to sixteen hundred and still be considered human? And his verbal was higher than his math. You can't do that if you're not at least marginally sapient, you know. He writes papers. He's no way nonverbal. He just doesn't interact socially."

I closed my eyes and thought about that face, that strange, empty face. All day, it looked like he did nothing but dream, somewhere away inside of himself. It gave me the creeps.

"He's inside there," Caulder went on, quietly. "I've known him all my life. He's inside there."

I thought about that. It reminded me of my grandmother, the way she was those last years in the nursing home. Her body was out of control and everybody just assumed that her mind was gone, too. But I always wondered if she was trapped in there somewhere . . . hearing everything, thinking her own thoughts. . . .

"So, do you, like, hang around with him, or what?"

He tossed his head around a little. "As much as you can, I guess," he said.

"And he's never said a word to you?"

"He's never so much as looked me straight in the eye."

"Never?" I asked him, incredulous.

"Not one time in seventeen years."

"Really. How could he live like that? What are his papers like? Have you ever read one?"

"A couple," he told me. "And let me tell you, the guy's mind is incredible. Very erudite. *Very.*"

"Did Mr. Leviaton really have him write an exam for the faculty?"

Caulder grinned. "Yeah. He did."

"That's amazing." I put my hands behind my head and stared up through the leaves. "That's just amazing."

"Yeah, well," Caulder said. "It's just as amazing to me." He smiled at me — a funny little mugging kind of smile.

"Are you hungry?" I asked him. "Because I am." I turned around and called the boys. I fixed Caulder with a stern look. "You have any money?" I asked him, because I've never believed in delicacy where money is concerned. "You want to share a pizza?"

"Can I bring my sisters?" he asked me. "They've been sitting back there on the porch all afternoon drooling over your brothers. That's why I came over here — they were making me sick."

So the six of us — three Pretigers and three Christiansons — all went out for pizza. And we had a great time. James talked engineering and Charlie talked music, and you could tell Caulder's sisters were just going to *love* living next door to us. And I wasn't exactly unhappy about the idea of being neighbors with Caulder.

So innocently can strange events begin.

CHAPTER TWO

"Why didn't you *tell* me you lived next door to the Pretigers?" Hally asked me at lunch the next day.

"I didn't know," I said. I opened the little Tupperware dish of sliced peaches my mother had sent in my lunch. "Why didn't you tell *me?*"

She leaned her chin on her hand and played around with her straw, dropping milk into her creamed corn, drip by drip.

"Want some?" I asked her, presenting my dish.

She nodded, and fished up a slip of peach with her spoon. "I've had a crush on Caulder Pretiger since first grade," she said, and the peach disappeared.

"I wonder why," I said, grinning.

She scowled at me, and then licked the spoon daintily. I offered her free access to the rest of my peaches. "You guys will probably get along just great," she said, not ungracefully, but with an edge of regret.

"We already do," I said, anticipating the look she gave me, and I grinned again. But then mercy got the best of me. "I have the feeling," I reassured her, "it's going to be a very fraternal relationship."

She squenched up her face and shook the spoon

19

at me. "Just make sure it *stays* that way."

A Ding Dong. My mother had put a *Ding Dong* in my lunch. Or maybe it was my dad making the lunches this morning.

"Actually," I said, peeling off the foil, "I've been thinking I ought to fall in love with Pete Zabriski."

She groaned.

"What? He's got the most wonderful eyes on the planet. *What?*"

"Are you actually serious?"

"Well, I mean — I just thought it would be fun. You know. And he *is* cute."

"He *is* cute," she allowed. "But guys like that never hang out with SADs."

"Pardon me?" I said.

"Scholastic and Academic Development program. Otherwise known as ultra honors." She rolled her eyes.

"This has some relevance to me?" I asked. "Because I don't know what you're talking about."

"You're in all SADs classes," she said. "Could you be honors and not know it?"

"I don't think so," I said. "Not with my math grades."

"Math," she agreed, grimacing. "I'm definitely a poet."

"Maybe it's all a mistake," I said, but I was thinking about my SAT scores, and all the tests my mother'd had run on us up at the university before we moved out here. Education is one of the Grand Christianson Obsessions. There've been whole years my mother's kept us home for intensive private study. As a result of that, Paul will perform the first brain transplant, James will someday build

20

a bridge across the Atlantic Ocean, Charlie — who is an actual musical genius — will probably end up writing the Great American Symphony, and I — I know a little bit about a lot of things.

I can tell you the chemical composition of the stuff you stick in your hair; how long it would take you, at just under the speed of light, to get to Alpha Centauri — and how old your body would be when you finally got there; the middle name of the third president of the United States; the amount of the present budget deficit; the author of *The Brothers Karamazov*; and how many feet there are in a line of trochaic heptameter. "*The Little Girl Who Had to Know Why,*" Paul used to call me. But even my mother couldn't reconcile me and math.

"I don't think they make that kind of mistake," Hally concluded. "Anyway — whether you're SADs or not, you're hanging around with SADs — me, for example — and that's death for dating. See, a smart woman tends to act on your typical eighteen-year-old male like instant kryptonite. But, not to worry — mother tells me something mystical happens at graduation and suddenly, male people who never pulled a grade above a C in their lives become automatically smarter than anything that wears a skirt. Maybe after that happens, we can date who we want."

"Well, like I say — I just thought it would be kind of fun," I sighed. "I mean, I never really expected him to take me out. I just thought it was so romantic that he plays the French horn. Whenever I hear the sound of a horn, I always get these visions of autumnal mists wafting through the Black Forest . . ."

21

"Oh, fine," she said, and she rolled her eyes again. "Give me your garbage, please. I believe it's time for me to take a trip to the can."

As dysfunctional as Smitty Tibbs was supposed to be, you'd expect him to walk around like some kind of robot or zombie or something — but that couldn't have been further from the truth. His movement was very normal, almost graceful. But he was moving through a world that didn't seem to admit the existence of any other human being.

Sometimes you'd hear people talking about him — *Who got the highest grade on the test? The Alien did.* Or, *Is this creamed corn going to kill me? I don't know — The Alien is eating it.* Stuff like that. It really was like he was living halfway in some other dimension, but I hated to hear that kind of talk; it kind of put the cap on his isolation. Not that he seemed to care.

I think he must have been kind of a challenge to my sense of reality, because I couldn't stop watching him. Maybe I thought, sooner or later, I was going to pick up on something that everybody else had missed. But Hally and Caulder were right. Watching Smitty Tibbs was like taking a little trip into the twilight zone. After a while, I had to make myself stop. It was really starting to bother me.

That's when Caulder decided he wanted to introduce us.

Oh, yes. Please. I could just see it: "Smitty — this is my friend Ginny — Ginny, Smitty — " and then what? "Nice to meet you?" Sure. Conversation with The Alien. One very big, creepy silence. No, no, no. Aliens are all right at a nice, objective distance; the idea of having him any closer gave me chills.

The thing about me is — essentially, I'm a coward.

I am. I can't stand weird stuff, anything that's not normal — mental illness and death and hospitals and pain and suffering and scary movies and people who need you and going into the basement alone at night (which Paul used to recommend I do, voluntarily, as a kind of self-therapy).

I'm a coward, and I've faced it, and I've learned to accept it. And I'm okay with that, as long as nothing happens so I have to start feeling ashamed about it, or guilty.

I don't think my parents know this about me. Or else, they must just refuse to accept the truth, because they keep treating me like I'm this mature, kind, generous, well-adjusted, generally courageous person. Or maybe it's just that they buy into all that Goethe stuff about having faith in people — thank you, philosophy.

But the other thing is, I just hate it when people are disappointed in me. I knew exactly what my parents would expect once they'd heard about Smitty: They'd expect me to do the decent thing. They'd expect me to befriend the kid. They'd probably want me to take him to the park every Saturday afternoon or something. Then they'd finally have to face the truth about their daughter, and they would definitely be disappointed, big time.

Because I wasn't going to do any of that. Not for a million bucks. I didn't want to go over to Smitty's house, I didn't want to take a walk in his moccasins, I didn't want to get involved with him, and I really didn't need anybody trying to shame me into it.

As for my folks, the solution was simple: I just didn't tell them about it. But Caulder was another thing altogether — Caulder, who was getting to be about the best friend I ever had, besides my family; Caulder, who had been almost single-handedly making the world a bearable place for me. I really didn't want him thinking less of me; I *really* wanted him to see that there were things I was good at. But he wouldn't let up on me. "Come on, Ginny. Just *meet* him." The pressure was terrible.

And who could I talk to about it, I ask you? Who would you go to for relief from your shame and your guilt? Once, I would have gone straight to Paul; *he* never had unrealistic expectations of me. *He* always tried to see my side of things. But that was before he'd gone brother *emeritus*, available only by phone. You'd think you could trust *all* your brothers to be that understanding, wouldn't you?

Of *course* you would.

Practically speaking, I knew I wasn't going to get any satisfaction out of Charlie; he's too sickeningly philanthropic. But James — James is like me, short on nobility, long on personal comfort. So I took a chance — on one of those long, solitary, parentless evenings, I opened my heart to my brother, James. I was being very honest and humble, and I should have known better.

"Selfish," James commented, before I had even finished. "So, you're scared of the guy." James has this annoying habit of going straight for the bottom line. "What — is he dangerous or something?"

24

"I never said he was dangerous." But then, I added, hopefully, "I guess he *could* be."

"Does he drool?"

My mouth dropped open. "Are you disgusting?" I said to him.

"Well, does he?"

"*No*. Of course not."

"Some people do," Charlie reminded us. "They can't help it."

"Thank you Charlie," I said, stiffly. "But that is *not* the point."

"The point is," James said, slipping down into the couch and putting his feet up on the coffee table, "you can't stand the thought of taking any kind of responsibility that's going to pull you outside of your little shell. You're scared to get close to the guy."

"So okay, I'm scared!" I yelled at him. "Why shouldn't I be scared? So — what, are you telling me you don't you think this whole thing is very weird? And what do you mean, 'shell'?"

"Would you like it if people were scared of you, just because you couldn't talk to them?" Charlie asked.

Oh, thank you, so very *much*.

"Did it ever occur to you people that he might *like* being alone?" I demanded, going for broke.

Charlie looked at me with gentle reproach. "I'll go over there with you, if you want."

"I'm not going *over* there. This is *not* what I wanted. What I *wanted* was a little sympathy. A little compassionate justification." I started gathering up my books. "Next time I have a pressing need to feel ashamed and guilty, I'll definitely know who to go to." I stalked out of the room, marched down the hall, slammed the door to my room, and didn't come out for the rest of the night.

Not that any of it helped. It wasn't like that door was going to keep out anything important. *"Turn it around,"* I could hear Paul saying, all the time, grinning. *"Imagine yourself into compassion."*

I sat there on my bed hating everything. I hated my father and his ideas. I hated Paul for growing up. I hated this town and Smitty Tibbs and my homeroom teacher and every other uncomfortable thing in the world. But most of all, I hated losing Caulder. Because I knew I was going to. People like him are too good for people like me. It would just be a matter of time till he found out the truth.

But if I'd known Caulder well enough, I could have saved myself a lot of soul-suffering.

It was just after that that Caulder decided it would be very good for us to start studying together. He'd come over after their family supper, spread his books all over our dining room table, and settle right in. The next night, James and Charlie drifted in, and then Caulder's sisters, Kaitlin and Melissa, and pretty soon there wasn't much room left at that table.

When we were all there, the house didn't seem so empty. The study sessions spilled over into the weekends, and then the six of us started doing things together — roller-skating and bowling and stuff. We made a religion out of Friday nights at the university's Classic Film Society — old movies are another one of the Christianson obsessions —

and every Sunday, we all went to Caulder's church.

"It's like having a big family," Charlie panted one day, throwing himself down onto the grass next to me. "Which is good, considering we actually do seem to be orphans." He and James had been playing badminton in the back with the girls until James and Kaitlin started arguing over some point of rule.

"I want to go home," I said, not bothering to lift my chin off the back of my hand.

"Not me," Charlie said, and rolled over on his back. "I love these trees. Have you noticed? The leaves are starting to turn. There's the thinnest line of yellow just starting on the edges. How long does it take, do you think, for the whole tree to turn? This whole street of trees. Ginny, it's going to be beautiful. We never had anything like that back home.

"Autumn," he went on, like he was tasting the word. "I've said it a million times, but I never knew what it meant before. Kind of scary, huh? You have to wonder how many other things you think you know, but you don't. I love this feeling in the air, this edge, like something is about to happen."

James was calling him. "I gotta go," he said, taking a gentle swipe at me.

I squinted up at the leaves, the sun coming down through a million tiny green stained-glass windows. I couldn't see any yellow till I stood up and took a single leaf in my hand. Charlie was right about that. You just had to look.

Caulder came out on his porch and leaned over the railing, one hand shading his eyes. "You seen the girls?" he called.

"In the back," I told him.

He nodded and waved. "Want to go over to Tibbs's?" he yelled, grinning.

"Not right now, thanks," I said, batting my eyes at him over clenched teeth.

"Later then," he said cheerfully, and he disappeared back into his house.

"In your dreams," I told him. He was gone by then.

One day very soon after that, Mrs. Shein, who believes in being cheerful instead of merciful, assigned us what she called a simple review problem — one of those totally cryptic review problems that you find triple starred at the end of a chapter. One look at it, and I knew I was dead.

I worked on it for hours that night. Caulder, Mr. Math Whiz, was no help at all — not because he couldn't solve it, mind you. Because he couldn't explain *how* he solved it. Caulder finally gave up completely, having chewed halfway through his pencil. But then, something dawned in his face, and he started grinning. "You've got it," I said, hopefully.

"I surely do," he said, and he stood up. "I know exactly where we can get help with this." I felt this terrible stab of foreboding. He pulled his coat off the back of his chair. "Come on," he said. "Get your stuff together."

"Just where are we going?" I asked, having this sinking feeling I already knew.

"Smitty's," he said, like it was the most natural thing in the world.

"Oh. Uh-huh," I said.

"I'm serious. He's more technical than I am. He

28

can explain this to you. I can't. Come on, Ginny. I'm not kidding."

So, what was I going to do? Short of throwing myself on the floor, I mean. Whatever else I may be, I do have my dignity. Caulder made me pack everything up, then he dragged me out the door and down the sidewalk, and there we were, standing on the Tibbses' front porch. My stomach was doing horrible loops.

"Hi, Mrs. Tibbs," Caulder said, when the door finally opened. Smitty's mother was a youngish-looking lady, very consciously dressed. "We've got a couple of math problems we can't quite nail down," Caulder explained, smiling. "We thought maybe Smitty could give us a hand."

She arched her eyebrows; evidently, this kind of thing didn't happen very often.

"We won't take too much of his time," Caulder assured her.

She looked doubtful. Actually, she looked at me, and *then* she looked doubtful. She pushed open the storm door. "Well," she said. "Come in."

We followed her into the living room, where there was this powder-blue carpet and a pale sofa with brocade upholstery. It was — I don't know — *perfect* in there, the kind of place you'd expect to find plastic runners on the floor. Like an ambassador's office or something.

She extended one hand, meaning we were supposed to sit down, which I did — but only on the very edge of the sofa cushion. I couldn't have vouched for the condition of the seat of my jeans, and I was terrified of leaving dusty smudges on that furniture.

29

"John," she said. There was a man sitting over in the corner behind a newspaper, half hidden by an open grand piano. "The children have come to see Smitty." She smiled at us and sat down across the room. "How is your mother, Caulder?" she asked. "I haven't seen her for a while."

"She's fine," Caulder said. "She's always got something going."

"Well . . ." Mrs. Tibbs said, and looked down at her watch and frowned. "John," she said, again. The newspaper didn't even rustle. Mrs. Tibbs sighed. "I have a meeting, and I'm running a little late . . ." she said to us.

"We're fine," Caulder said, not giving an inch. "We just need to see Smitty for a minute."

She was clearly undecided as to what she should do with us. The newspaper shifted, came halfway down. "John," she said. "Caulder's here." It was the big man from the driveway. He gave us a not unfriendly glance and a nod. "They want to see Smitty," she went on.

"He's upstairs," Mr. Tibbs said.

"I *know* he's upstairs," she said. "They want to ask him about some — what was it, Caulder?"

"Math, Mrs. Tibbs." Caulder was being very polite.

"Math," she repeated, looking at her husband.

He looked at her blankly. It was like she was trying to get him to say something, but he didn't have the faintest idea what she wanted.

She gave her husband a long look and then turned back to us. "I'm not sure what you think he can do," she said. "Of course, I'll call him down for you — but Caulder — "

"We just have a few questions, Mrs. Tibbs. You know you don't have to worry about me." Caulder patted my trig book and smiled at her again.

"Well," she said. "I'd love to stay and help you myself, but I do have my meeting . . ." She stood up. "Just don't upset him," she said. And then, quickly, "Of course, Caulder, I know you never would. Why don't you two go on into the dining room where you can work, and I'll go up and get Smitty. Then I'll have to go — "

"We'll be fine, thank you," Caulder said. He got up and so I got up. We followed Mrs. Tibbs out of the room and went in through a door she opened for us.

"Just make yourselves comfortable," she said, reaching in for the light switch. A small but brilliant chandelier flamed to life. She closed the door softly behind us.

"Sit here," Caulder told me. I pulled out a chair and sat down. These chairs were awfully formal, but at least they were wooden, and I didn't have to worry about making a mess out of them.

I think I must have been wringing my hands or something.

"Come on," Caulder said, cuffing me on the arm. "Relax."

I dropped my jaw and gaped at him. "Relax," I repeated. I sat on my hands and started looking around the room. The first thing you had to notice was this big portrait on the wall — Mr. and Mrs. Tibbs and Smitty and another kid, older than Smitty, but somewhat like him — all sitting there looking very beautiful inside this heavy wood-and-gold frame.

"So, Smitty's got a brother?" I asked. I don't know why that surprised me so much.

"More or less," Caulder said.

Before I had a chance to ask him what *that* was supposed to mean, Mrs. Tibbs put her head in at the door. "He'll be down in a minute. Now Caulder — "

"We won't be long," Caulder said. "Thank you, Mrs. Tibbs."

She smiled, but you could tell she still wasn't entirely comfortable with the situation. Fine. She wasn't the only one. "Good night," she said. And then she disappeared. We looked at each other and rolled our eyes. A moment later, we heard the front door close.

And then Smitty Tibbs came in and sat down.

I jumped.

I hadn't heard a sound. One minute we were alone, the next, he was there, pulling out a chair for himself.

He was wearing glasses — round lenses with thin tortoiseshell frames. They looked kind of old-fashioned and jaunty. It was weird to see something jaunty on that empty, beautiful face.

"This is Ginny," Caulder said. "She's not real bright, but she's my friend."

I kicked him under the table.

"I'm only kidding," Caulder said, rather melo-dramatically rubbing at his shin. "Actually, she's kind of bright. Not overwhelmingly. We just have this problem with these problems." He went on for another minute, explaining things. I just sat there, staring at Smitty. I figured it was okay to stare — it wasn't as if he was going to *see*. His eyes were fixed . . . well, not really fixed. He wasn't staring. He was just kind of absently looking — like when you lose yourself in your thoughts. Anyway, it seemed like his attention was lost on something across the room — his mother's hutch, maybe.

Caulder nudged me. "Do the problem," he said. "Show him."

"I can't *do* the problem," I whined.

"*Show* him," Caulder said to me, keeping his teeth very close together.

So I flipped open my notebook — not very gracefully — dragged out the assignment sheet, found the diagram in my book, and explained to the human void sitting next to me just exactly what the problem was. I was thinking this was about the stupidest, most useless thing I had ever done in my life.

Until he moved that stare from his mother's hutch to my paper.

So, he was listening.

Of course, he did it like — *Oh. What's this I just noticed on my dining room table by accident* — *? Gosh, I wonder how it got there.* Not that he seemed surprised. He never seemed anything.

Finally, I finished. I sat there, waiting. All the echoes of my voice settled out of the air, and I was beginning to get the uncanny feeling I'd never really spoken at all.

Smitty Tibbs pulled the book a little closer. Then he reached for my notebook, removed a blank piece of paper, picked up a pencil — all very simple movements, and unself-conscious, as if he were all alone in the whole world. He tapped the diagram lightly with the eraser of the pencil.

He began to do the problem. He went through it slowly, writing everything — documentation, theorems, and corollaries — in detail, taking no shortcuts, with absolutely no abbreviations, no assumptions — and he did it in this very clean, precise printing that reminded me of my dad's architectural hand.

I began to forget who he was, watching him work. I got lost in the logic, in reading the things he'd written — all very technical, precise. Of course, I got thoroughly confused. Without thinking, I said ". . . but . . ."

His hand stopped.

Then I remembered where I was. And I got embarrassed.

"What's the problem?" Caulder asked me.

It wasn't something I could explain. I just hadn't understood — it was a connection I hadn't made, a logical fault.

Smitty Tibbs waited a moment longer. When I didn't say anything more, he went back to work — only, he started a few steps above where he'd stopped, going back over what he'd already done — this time, tracing out each line on the diagram as he worked with it. I'd had to have been blind not to see what he was doing. When he finally finished that proof, even an idiot would have understood it.

Therefore, I understood.

I understood a lot of things.

Caulder was right, for one.

There was something inside of there.

* * *

"So what about his brother?" I asked Caulder as soon as we were out of that house. "Is he like Smitty? Or is he normal?"

Caulder laughed. "He's not like Smitty," he said, rubbing his hands together and blowing on them against the night chill. And then he studied me, as though he were trying to read my soul. "I can tell you a little bit more about Smitty," he said, finally. "If you're interested."

As if I could be anything else, now.

Caulder grinned to himself.

"None of this is common knowledge," he said. I nodded. "Just so you understand." I nodded again. "Smitty was actually normal till he was about two. Then one day, Smitty's mom took her kids to the community pool, and Smitty fell asleep in the sun. So she covered him up with towels, and went in swimming. I guess it never crossed her mind he wouldn't be okay."

"She left a two-year-old alone at a *pool?*" The voice that came out of my mouth might have been my mother's.

"I know," Caulder said, shrugging. "I guess she took it for granted somebody would notice him if he woke up and started wandering round — there are tons of people at that pool all the time. Or maybe she left him with Russell. Anyway, later, when the lifeguard pulled Smitty out of the pool, he was just about drowned. Actually, he was dead."

Caulder pulled his collar up under his ears. "But they got him resuscitated, and he was in the hospital for quite a while before he went home. He never said another word after that. At first, they

35

thought it was the trauma, that it'd wear off eventually. Later, they figured it must be permanent brain damage. Smitty's dad was really broken up about it; my dad says he got real quiet after that. Anyway, it never should have happened."

"Amen," I whispered.

After a moment, he added, "Smitty doesn't seem real damaged to me."

I was inclined to agree with that, too. Two minutes, maybe, it had taken him to work out that proof.

"Maybe it's just the outside," I said. "Maybe it's just like the outside layer of him isn't functional. Like his facial nerves don't work. Maybe he just somehow lost connection with his language centers, and he can't communicate."

"Or like, he *won't*," Caulder said.

I laughed.

He looked at me and made no comment.

"You seriously think it's just a matter of his refusing to speak?" I asked. "Refusing to speak for fifteen *years*? Not likely."

"It's a mystery," Caulder intoned. He grinned at me. I could have smacked him one; I know self-satisfaction when I see it. But then, he had every reason to be satisfied — he'd finally found himself a partner.

From that night on, I was just as obsessed with Smitty as he was.

CHAPTER
THREE

It took some getting used to, walking with
Caulder and Smitty. You try to carry on a normal
conversation — you try to be polite so nobody
feels left out. I never realized before then how
much of my conversation comes out in questions.
I never realized before how important it is to have
people *answer* you. Being with Smitty Tibbs for even
the barest modicum of time, you could start doubting your own reality.

The only thing we actually knew about him for
sure was that he was standing there. That's not
enough for human beings — we have to know
what people are thinking, and why and how they're
going to jump. So naturally, I caught myself making
up personalities for him — you know, the way you
do with pets and cute boys and famous people.
What's that called? *Anthropomorphism.* You do it so
that you feel you can relate personally to whatever
it is — your dog, or God, or whatever. You do
that so you can care about things, and so that life
at least appears to make sense. And maybe you do
it so you can feel like something cares about you.

"The dangerous thing about doing that," Paul told me
one time, *"is what you end up caring about isn't necessarily
what's really there — just what you've decided is there.*

Which may be very far from the truth. So you could very easily end up depending on a lie. Or a dream."

I didn't want to do that with Smitty; I wanted to keep a very scientific attitude toward the whole thing. So I tried to unravel him by concentrating on the hard evidence — the way he dressed, for instance — Caulder *had* said that Smitty chose his own clothes. And the fact that Smitty's work was neat and methodical. But then, computers are neat and methodical. Also, I figured, anybody who could be willing to help me with my math night after night — we were going over there practically every night of the week, now — must be truly nice. And patient.

So anyway, he had conservative taste, and he was nice and patient.

Or maybe not.

So for me to say that Smitty Tibbs had been walking to school *with* us would be pushing a point. Every morning now, Smitty came out of his house, strolled down his front path to the sidewalk, and walked to school. Caulder, who had been waiting at the foot of his own front path for maybe several minutes, would fall in beside Smitty, and then as the two of them came by my house, I, having stood at the foot of *my* walk for at least thirty seconds — would fall in with them in turn, and so we all got to school. On a good day, it looked like a Blue Angels flight maneuver.

Of course, we'd never had any way of telling whether Smitty was pleased with the arrangement. "As long as he doesn't let us know how he feels," Caulder would say, "we get to assume what we want."

Which I've already explained wasn't good enough for me. So, I took up vigil once again. I wanted to catch something — the slightest flicker of an expression, the slightest reaction. I wanted to see him scratch his nose, or stumble and look sheepish, or puzzled or angry. I wanted to see some evidence that he was actually *human*.

I kind of missed being able to talk all this stuff over with my mom. We used to like trying to figure things out together. There was presently no chance of that, so I pretty much had to be satisfied with Caulder. Which was okay — he had a level head, and I trusted his judgment. Mostly.

"Look," I said to him sweetly one afternoon. "Since you were so kind as to introduce me to *your* friend, why don't you let me introduce you to one of mine?"

Evidently, in our relationship, total trust was not a reciprocal thing. Caulder gave me a look that was definitely suspicious and began to edge away.

"Yeah?" he said. "And just who might you have in mind?"

"How come you never go out?" I asked, bluntly.

"I go out," he said, indignantly. "I go out with you all the time."

"I mean with girls," I said — for once, pushing aside the obvious implications. He spluttered. "What a jerk," I said. "I suppose you're going to tell me you're shy."

"I *am* shy," he said. "I've always been shy."

I gave him a sidelong look of pure disgust.

"*All* the Pretigers are shy," he said, huffily.

"You should have asked Hally out years ago," I said.

His mouth dropped open. "Forget it," he said.

"What do you mean, 'forget it'?" I asked. "You guys'd make a swell couple."

"Ginny," he said carefully, as though he were talking to some kind of idiot, "have you looked at me lately? I mean, really looked? You think somebody like Hally would ever go out with somebody like me? She would never take a second look at me."

All of a sudden, a little light went on in my brain. "You like her, don't you?" I asked him, mildly amazed.

He nodded, dumbly.

"So, how come you never said anything?"

"I don't have to tell you everything," he pointed out, making a sad little grab at dignity.

Then I got a little perverse (which happens more often than you might think). "You never asked her out because she's smart. That's it, isn't it?" I said. "You're one of those guys who has to have an airheaded, adoring little girlfriend who doesn't threaten you. Caulder, I can't believe this — you're scared to go out with her because you might find out she's more intelligent than you. I am *so* disappointed."

He glared at me. "And you are *so* wrong."

I folded my arms and gave him a long look. "So prove it."

"I don't have to prove it," he huffed, "and I don't want to talk about it anymore."

I laughed my head off, and then we started talking about something else. But if he thought the subject was closed, he had another thing coming.

40

* * *

The next night I got us into trouble. It was really Caulder's fault; he should have warned me. Well, there are times when maturity seems to evaporate. When otherwise perfectly responsible, disciplined people get a little silly, maybe, and suddenly everything is hilariously funny. You try — you say, "Okay, guys — we have to get serious now . . ." and everybody genuinely tries to get back to work. You try to keep your mind on what you're doing. You try not to *think* about laughing — but then somebody slips and lets out a half-strangled sputter and everything totally falls apart.

I love it when that happens.

I don't know what set us off this particular night, but it got bad. We were just so funny. I was having a great time until I came up against these trig problems that were definitely *not* amusing — not even accessible to the normal human mind — especially when I realized that Mrs. Shein wasn't going to think it was so funny when I handed her nothing but my name and an apology next day. Definitely material for Tibbs's Tutorial.

Maybe we shouldn't have gone over there until we'd sobered up.

We managed to maintain perfect maturity while we were standing in Mrs. Tibbs's presence. I did get a little crazy for a minute, though, and I actually talked directly to her: I asked her where she was going. It was an honest question; it seemed like every time we came in, she was just going out.

She looked kind of pleased that I should ask. "Actually," she said, checking her watch, "I'm a little late. I'm treasurer for Child Rescue, and we meet

41

every other Tuesday. You know about Child Rescue?"

I had to admit that I didn't. I was, however, *very* aware that Caulder was looking at me like I'd lost my mind.

"Well, we're a philanthropic organization dedicated to protecting children from inner-city areas — lower-income groups — from various kinds of abuse. We have a shelter that we operate downtown. We've done some wonderful things. Maybe sometime, you'd like to do some volunteer work down at the shelter?"

"Maybe next summer," I said, backing up half a step. Among my other faults, I'm not very good at commitment on short notice.

"Let me tell you — here's Smitty — if you have the time, and you're willing, there's a lot of good you can do out there." She smiled, shouldered her purse, and opened the front door. "Enjoy yourselves." She hesitated with her hand on the doorknob. "It's nice that Smitty has some friends," she said, and then she closed the door behind her.

Suddenly, I wasn't feeling so silly anymore.

"Get in here," Caulder said, and hauled me into the dining room by the shoulder of my sweater.

Smitty followed us in, just the way he always did — like he'd suddenly gotten the urge to go and sit in the dining room and do the math that just sort of mysteriously appeared there every night.

It was all so ridiculous. I started trying to explain why I didn't understand the first problem, but I got all mixed up and, after a few minutes, I could hear Caulder starting up again out of the corner of my ear. I couldn't look straight at him because I was afraid I'd start cracking up, too.

He sat over there spluttering to himself from time to time, and every time he did, I had to stop and take a careful breath. My stomach muscles were starting to cramp from being held in so tightly. My cheeks were stiff.

We were *trying* not to be impolite. The harder we tried, the worse it got. Finally, I was sitting there with my fists crammed into my eyes and tears running down my face, and Caulder was practically lying on the table. We couldn't stop.

After what had to have been several minutes, Smitty folded his hands and put them in his lap, a fairly definite indication that he was tired of us. I became very contrite and sobered right up. Caulder was a little bit slower on the uptake, but finally it was very quiet in the room. Smitty picked up the pencil again and leaned forward to write.

"Sorry," Caulder said. "I can tell you think we're nuts . . ."

For a fraction of a second, just a shade of a moment, Smitty froze.

". . . but we really don't mean to be a pain."

Smitty blinked a couple of times, and then he went back to work on the problem, while I was still sitting there, trying to figure out why I felt like lightning had just struck. Of course, I missed half of the explanation.

"Wait," I said, and I put my hand on Smitty's arm.

He put the pencil down, shoved himself away from the table, got up, and left the room.

I looked at Caulder, then I stared at Smitty's

chair, then I turned around and looked at the door. He was actually gone. He'd just suspended operations and left.

"Did I do something?" I asked Caulder.

"Come on," he said, philosophically. He started gathering things up. "I'll help you with this stuff at home. Let's go."

We let ourselves out, quietly.

"You touched him," Caulder said, answering my question. "I should have told you — nobody's allowed to do that. Not even his parents." I was humiliated. Completely. "Not your fault," Caulder commented, breathing out a tiny cloud of steam.

I stopped dead in the middle of the sidewalk, staring at my feet.

Caulder turned around and looked at me. "What?" he said. "I told you it wasn't your fault."

"No," I said, suddenly breathless. "Something just happened in there."

"Yeah," Caulder said. "We acted like a couple of idiots."

"Not that," I told him. "Something — look. Why did he leave the room?"

Caulder made an exasperated little sound. "I told you; he doesn't allow touching."

"Okay, then why did he put his hands in his lap? When we were laughing?"

"Because we were being obnoxious."

"And when you apologized — when you said, 'I can tell you think we're nuts'? — he, like, just suddenly stopped for a second, like you'd shocked him."

"So?" Caulder said, but he was thinking now, too.

"So, aren't those reactions? He was reacting to us. We didn't realize it at the time — but we responded to it, just the way we would have responded to anybody else. It was almost like a conversation. Don't you get it?"

Caulder blinked. "I'm starting to." He was breathing a little faster.

"Maybe he's getting used to us or something. Or maybe we're just finally seeing what's always been there."

"No," Caulder said, looking back at Smitty's house. "Not what's always been there." Then he stuffed his hands into his pockets and buried his chin in the collar of his jacket. He blinked again. "Why now?" he asked, looking up at me. "It's gotta just be that we're trying too hard. We're seeing what we want to see."

"You really think that?" I asked him, impatiently.

"Ginny," he said. "I don't know how to think anything else." He shook his head. "What if — no. I just don't know how to think anything else. Come on. I'm freezing." He started to walk. I wanted to kick him, but instead I fell in beside him, seething. "If something has actually changed," he went on, very carefully, "then we're bound to see more of it. We've just got to stay objective, but stay aware. Okay? Objective, but aware."

"Fine," I said, more than a little disappointed in his sense of drama.

He stopped at the bottom of my walk, waiting for me to go up first. Then he followed me, still looking very thoughtful. "If what you say turns out to be true . . ." he said as he climbed up the porch steps and reached past me for the doorknob, ". . . the universe just reeled on its axis."

Suddenly, he grinned at me and pushed the front door open. "Okay, you guys," he yelled. "We can hear you breathing in there. I hope you've gotten some serious work done."

Of course, they hadn't.

CHAPTER FOUR

September was half gone, and our street was going up in flames. It was strange — where I come from, trees are mostly green, and then they turn brown; after that, the leaves come off and it rains a little bit. That's when you have to start wearing long-sleeved T-shirts in the evening. But here, the nights go chill, and then the trees turn themselves inside out, gold and russet and scarlet all mixed with fading green, like something out of Alice's looking glass.

Charlie loved it, of course. His sense of security is anchored in more abstract things than the colors of leaves. And I have to admit, I thought it was beautiful, too — in an unsettling kind of way.

I retreated to the house, but kept bumping into corners and bookcases that stuck out in places where I didn't expect them. The good old couches and piano and dining room furniture were there, but they seemed strangely disjointed in their new, raw rooms. All of the softening things, the pictures and the little homey stuff — all the evidence that real human beings were living and breathing in this space — were still packed away in boxes and crates, stacked against one wall of the den.

Sometimes I would suddenly remember how the

afternoon sunlight used to lie on the floor of the hall just outside my old room, and I'd feel a terrible longing for home.

While nights were chilly, the days were warm, sometimes hot. My parents were making headway on the studio, but it was slow going. When Paul called one night, the sound of his voice was like an echo of a dream.

In the mornings, I'd look at myself in the mirror and wonder. It was the same face, the same dark eyes and unrepentant hair, but the feelings were not familiar, and the face seemed a little like a mask. I needed some Romance, maybe, to take my mind off things and put a little color in the face. The people at school were all nice enough, but nobody'd asked me out, yet. That made me a little sad; I couldn't help thinking about how much fun I'd always had at home. Maybe everybody was thinking Caulder and I were a serious item. Maybe that's why nobody was taking me seriously.

It was in front of the mirror one morning that I finally decided, Hally or no Hally, I was going to go ahead and have a crush on Pete Zabriski. Actually, it hadn't bothered me at all, what she'd said about him; I've always believed you can get a lot more emotional mileage out of a love-from-afar kind of a relationship than the real flesh-and-blood kind. I mean, if you never get close to anybody, you don't have to be disappointed in them. And real relationships can get so messy, especially when the other person wants to put more into them than you do. Or vice versa.

No, a hopeless heartthrob was perfect for me.

Evidently, Caulder was of my ilk. Every day, I

had Hally on one side, asking little leading questions, making wistful observations — hints, all of them — and Caulder on the other not wanting to talk about it. I was getting very impatient with him, and you can believe I didn't exactly hide that fact.

Maybe I should have left well enough alone.

Our Friday-Night-Christianson/Pretiger-Lonely-Hearts-Outings at the film society had turned out to be very culturally broadening. In those first few weeks, we'd seen *The Treasure of the Sierra Madre* — which I'd already seen once with Paul when we used to stay up for the Midnight Movie Classics of the Week — *It Happened One Night*, and *Meet John Doe*. My mom always made a very big deal about these films when we told her about them; my mother's Favorite Movie is just about anything made before 1953. When she heard we were going to see *The Heart is a Lonely Hunter* — which I told her about one morning as she was heading out the door — she clutched her heart and rolled her eyes and generally let me know it was going to be a winner, without managing to communicate anything remotely specific.

So we were kind of looking forward to seeing it. But on that Friday morning, both Charlie and James came down with the flu. Kaitlin and Melissa, of course, were suddenly overcome with fits of Florence Nightingale. Caulder and I should really have been more sympathetic than restless, but that's not the way it worked out.

"Look," James groaned finally. "All we want to do is lie around here and watch TV, and you know how superior you guys get when the TV's on. So why don't you just make us all happy and go away?"

"We have actually been paid," Kaitlin informed us, "for taking care of people far more helpless than these two. It's not like we need you two around supervising." To prove a point, Melissa stuck a thermometer into Charlie's mouth. "Go," Charlie mouthed around it, "before they kill us."

So, we went.

"So," Caulder said as we got into the car. "We could take Smitty."

That was kind of a shocking idea.

"To the *movies?*" Mrs. Tibbs repeated, standing in the doorway, looking more than slightly incredulous.

"Sure," Caulder said. "We're just going up to the university, and we thought Smitty might like to tag along. It's no big thing. It's just Friday night." He flashed her the patented Caulder-is-so-mature smile.

"Caulder," Mrs. Tibbs said, quietly, "I think you're forgetting that Smitty has some very serious limitations."

"I never forget that," he said.

"I appreciate the interest you've taken in Smitty, honey. But I have to be honest — I'm just not comfortable with the idea of him going with you — not that I don't trust you, Caulder. I just don't think you understand what can happen."

"We'll take care of him," Caulder said, simply. "He's eighteen, Mrs. Tibbs. He's an honor student."

Mrs. Tibbs shifted her weight and sighed, looking off over our shoulders into her own thought. "John," she started to call, leaning back into the hall. But she bit the name off, murmuring to herself.

"I really don't think you have to worry. He goes to high school with us every day," Caulder said, sounding very reasonable.

She took a deep breath. "Well —"

"We won't be back too late," Caulder said. "We won't take him out anywhere afterward."

"How much is it?" she asked, and then we knew she was going to let him go.

"It's just the film society," Caulder told her. "It's just a buck-and-a-half."

Ten minutes later, Smitty was belted into the backseat of Caulder's father's car, going to the movies just like a normal person. Whether he was pleased about it or not, who could tell? It was strange for us, having him back there, and we were a little self-conscious at first. But we loosened up after a bit; he was so quiet, we nearly forgot he was there.

We had to park down the hill from campus and hike up to the building, and then we had to wait in line with three hundred other people in a narrow hallway for forty-five minutes. The whole time, Smitty Tibbs stood beside us, pretending he was alone in the world. If that's what he was doing.

Finally, we paid for Smitty's ticket, herded him along into the auditorium, found three seats together, sat down and broke out our goodies. I leaned over and put a Snickers on the arm of Smitty's seat, being careful not to touch him, and then the lights went off and the movie started.

I guess I should have made Mom tell me more.

Alan Arkin plays the main character, a deaf-mute man who takes a room with a southern family during the Depression. The family is down on their luck, the father disabled and money scarce, which is why they had to take in a boarder. It's a movie about poverty and anger and handicaps and love — the spiritual and physical traps human beings can fall into. Not what you'd call light entertainment.

I was uncomfortable at first, wondering if the handicaps of the protagonist were going to upset Smitty. But when he didn't show any signs of distress, I forgot all about him and lost myself in the story. That's what I love about good films, and good books — you can climb right into them and be there. I just hate it when I'm doing that, and then somebody butts in and messes with my concentration.

Which some idiot did right in the middle of the climax of the movie. An innocent person had been brutally hurt, and Alan Arkin was the only one who knew. He had to get help, but no one could understand him — he was trapped inside of that body, and the horrible sounds that tore their way out of his throat took you by the heart and ripped you apart. It was not the best time for somebody to decide they needed to climb over me to get to the aisle.

"Where's he going?" Caulder whispered.

"*What?*" I snapped. But I noticed that the seat on the other side of Caulder was empty. So my idiot had been Smitty.

"Who knows?" I hissed back. "To the bathroom. How should *I* know?"

"Yeah, maybe that's where he went," Caulder said, doubtfully. He craned his neck around, looking back toward the door. Then he shrugged. "He's probably just . . ." He shrugged again and settled back into his seat.

I tried to get back into the movie. But I kept waiting for Smitty to come back, and so did Caulder. Every so often, we'd look at each other and feel uncomfortable.

Then it was over. "I'm exhausted," Caulder said, and I could only agree. We looked for Smitty as we left the auditorium. There were hundreds of people waiting for the next show, lines looped all up and down the hall. We didn't see Smitty there. Caulder checked out the men's room. No Smitty. We went through the whole building, and then we decided he must be waiting for us at the car. So we went all the way down to the parking lot, only to find out that he wasn't there — so we had to go back to the building.

By this time, the halls were empty and the next show was running. Caulder talked the kid at the door into letting him go in to see if maybe Smitty had wandered back in there, looking for us. Which he evidently hadn't.

We checked out every crevice of the building, the entire grounds around the building, half the campus, and then we went down and got the car. We drove home slowly, watching both sides of the street all the way — no Smitty.

"His mother's gonna freak," Caulder muttered. He turned the car around and drove back to the university another way. Then we started driving a grid — back and forth, every possible street. It was getting very late. And Caulder was starting to get seriously scared. I was worried, too — but Caulder was nearly frantic.

Well, we finally did find Smitty. He was walking down our own street, just passing in front of Caulder's house. Caulder pulled in hard against the curb, jumped out of the car, came around, and put a hand out. Smitty stopped. Then Caulder started yelling, not so loud Mrs. Tibbs would have heard it, but loud enough I could hear, outlining in great detail the extent of our search and generally sounding a whole lot like my father.

"You just don't do that to people," Caulder said, finally losing some steam.

But Smitty Tibbs hadn't heard a word of it. Caulder stepped out of his way, and Smitty went home.

Then Caulder got back into the car and slid down in the seat, his head back against it, sighing. He looked at me. Neither of us said anything. He started the car, pulled into his driveway, and turned off the ignition, all without a word.

"You want to come over?" I asked him. I was feeling kind of worn-out and cross. Maybe a little tired of the game.

"It's late," he said. We got out of the car. He stood there on the driveway, looking over toward Smitty's house. A light had just gone on upstairs. "Sometimes," Caulder said, "I think this is going to drive me crazy. He's probably sitting up there in his room, making faces at himself in the mirror and laughing his head off."

"Why do you do this?" I asked him. "It's not your job to baby-sit Smitty Tibbs. Why don't you just let him take care of himself?"

He turned to me and blew a little cloud of steam into the night air. "I suppose you thought we should

54

have just gone home and left him?"

"No," I said. "Of course not." I stuck my hands into the pockets of my jacket. "It's just — who made you his keeper? I mean, we could have just gone to the movie without him, tonight. It was *your* idea to take him. What did you think was going to happen?"

"I don't know," he said. "Maybe I just thought he'd like a little chance. Just to live, you know? I'm not his keeper." He looked back over his shoulder at Smitty's house. "I'm his friend."

I don't know what went through my mind just then — a thousand things mostly having to do with my concept of friendship, and the fact that, I guess, I never really thought of Smitty as an actual human being. And maybe some jealousy. "I thought, to be friends, you had to really know each other. A relationship," I said, finally. "Like you and me."

"Yeah," he said. "Well, it's never going to be like you and me, is it?" He sighed, and mist curled around his face. "I can't explain it to you," he said to me. "How can you explain why you love somebody?"

"You love him? You don't even *know* him. You don't even know if there's anybody in there to *love*."

He laughed. "Do you ever really know anybody?" he asked, and I shivered in the dark. "Go home," Caulder said. "I'll see you tomorrow. I'll watch you to your door."

He was still standing there when I climbed my steps and put my hand on the knob. I gave him a little wave. "And I love you, too," he called to me. He was gone before I could answer.

The girls were gone. Only Charlie was still up, all wrapped up in his plaid robe with my mom's slippers on his feet. He was sitting at the piano as I locked the door behind me, softly playing the adagio from Beethoven's *Pathetique* sonata.

I took off my coat and hung it in the closet, then I bumped him over and sat beside him on the bench.

"Don't get too close," he warned, leaning away so he wouldn't breathe on me.

"Mom and Dad home yet?" I asked.

"Of course not," he said.

I sighed. "This is not cheerful music," I told him.

"It's loving music," he said, closing his eyes as he played. "It's gentle."

As he played, I looked around the sterile living room. "I wonder if this could ever end up seeming like home," I said, softly.

He looked at me and smiled. "As the prophet said — 'No man, having put his hand to the plow, and looking back, is fit for the kingdom.'"

"Oh, that's helpful," I said, and I got up.

"Be happy, Ginny," he told me. He dropped his hands into his lap and turned to face me. "This is home. This is where we are. This is the place we store our love. You just have to be content to be in your own skin, that's all. And I think I'm going to throw up. Again."

He slid off the bench and headed for the bathroom. I listened to make sure he was going to make it, then I took one more look around. I started shutting off lights and checking windows. I'd wanted to ask Charlie a question. I'd wanted to ask

him — "Do you think we really know each other?
Any of us?"

I left one light on, the little lamp on the piano,
so my parents would have something warm to come
home to.

CHAPTER FIVE

So, the very next afternoon, here's Caulder, squinting up against the sunlight at Smitty's curtained windows and telling me, "I think it's worth another try."

It was actually funny to me, at that point. "Sure," I said. "We had such a *great* time last night."

"Ginny," Caulder said, "I'm serious. I've been thinking a lot about that stuff you said the other night, when Smitty walked out on us at his house. I was thinking — he walked out on us again at the university, didn't he? I mean, we don't know why he did it, but he did do it, and I believe there had to have been a reason. Maybe we could figure it out if we gave it another try. It might really turn out to be important."

So, on Friday night, while everybody else went to a Dave Gruisin concert in the city, Caulder and I went to Smitty's for math. On the way out, we mentioned to Mrs. Tibbs that we were going to the movies again, and said we'd love to take Smitty along.

She didn't argue at all. It struck me that Mrs. Tibbs might actually be seeing this as an advantage; when Smitty was with us, she could do whatever it was she did without feeling guilty. So, one minute, Smitty was standing in his front hall; the next, he had his coat on and was climbing into the backseat of the car. No one had asked his opinion.

We kept a close eye on him this time. Even after we were sitting down, Smitty carefully between us, we were uneasy.

The movie was *East of Eden* — John Steinbeck and James Dean. That — and the fact that my mother thought this was a great classic — was the sum total of what I knew about it, which was enough; I could have guessed it wasn't going to be real funny.

What an understatement.

East of Eden turned out to be a sort of dust bowl Cain and Abel story — set in the rural American midwest about sixty years ago. The Abel brother was good and virtuous and hardworking, and everybody loved him. The Cain brother was misunderstood, and therefore resentful, envious, and violent. One perfect — the other not able to please anybody, including himself. You didn't really get to side with anybody because you had to grieve for all. Fun. A real fun experience.

About two thirds of the way through, there was an accident, and the Abel brother was killed. That was when Smitty decided to leave. We couldn't do anything but follow him, trying to keep up — out of the building, down the hill — Caulder all the time saying, "Wait up. Will you wait up?"

But Smitty was gone. He was disappearing into the shadows at the foot of the parking lot when Caulder finally came to a stop, puffing. I had started slowly across the lot toward the car, watching them from above.

"Smitty," Caulder yelled.

Smitty didn't stop.

"Fine," Caulder called. "What am I going to tell your mother?" But he might as well have been calling to the moon.

"Okay," he finally shouted. "So, you're upset. So, you're mad at us. We get the message, *okay?*"

Smitty Tibbs stopped. Stopped dead in his tracks.

He was suspended in the shadows. Still. Completely silent. Then, all at once, he turned and started back up the lot toward the car, as if he'd suddenly remembered where he was going. Caulder glanced back at me, but I could only shrug.

Then Caulder headed for the car, himself. I was nearly there, so I stopped and waited for them. I saw Smitty clearly as he toiled on up the slope and passed through the brightness below the streetlights.

I saw him *very* clearly, in fact.

"Come on," Caulder said, closer to me than I'd expected. He took my arm and steered me over to the car.

I'd seen glittering tracks of silver on Smitty's face in that half-light. I felt like somebody'd knocked the wind out of me.

Smitty was tucked away in the shadows of the backseat by the time Caulder opened my door for me. I climbed in and put the belt on, my heart thudding, and then I sat with my hands in my lap, feeling very chilly and almost dizzy.

Caulder threw himself into his seat and jammed his belt into place. "I swear to you, Smitty," he said, adjusting the rearview mirror, "your mother would literally *kill* me if she thought I let you get away like that. Do you know what can happen to people walking around alone in the dark in this town? You get away with an awful lot, buddy, but you're not going to pull this kind of thing on me." He jammed the car into gear, pulled out of the lot, and onto the street.

There wasn't a sound from the backseat.

I couldn't say anything. I was still too cold. Caulder gave me a curious look. I couldn't meet his eyes.

Smitty Tibbs had just graduated from Interesting Problem to full, frighteningly real, Human Being.

Caulder pulled up into his own driveway, and I was out of the car before he'd pulled on the parking brake. Smitty took the opening and flew — gone before Caulder could open his own door. I watched him disappear across Caulder's lawn, his shadow flitting behind him, and then I leaned over, put the back of my seat right, and looked at Caulder.

Caulder slammed his palms against the wheel.

"So you were right," I said to him. "You should be happy."

He looked at me. "No," he said. "We didn't learn anything."

"Caulder," I said, softly. "Didn't you see it?"

"See what?" he asked. "I see that The Alien can't sit through an entire movie. I see that some people don't have any sense at all — he doesn't even know the way *home*."

"He got home okay the other night," I pointed out, gently. "Caulder — "

"Maybe you're right," he said, not hearing me.

61

"Maybe I've spent a lot of years for nothing."

"Caulder — " I said again. He shook his head and glared at me. I held up one hand, asking for just a tiny break in his frustration.

"What?" he said, finally.

"Caulder," I said, gently, "he was crying."

Caulder's face didn't change much at all but, suddenly, he was staring. He'd gone sort of hollow, moving slowly past shock and into disbelief.

"I saw it when he was coming to the car."

"It was dark," he said.

I shook my head. "I know what I saw."

Caulder's eyes glazed over — he'd gone completely inside himself, and his breathing quickened. "You're sure?" he said, coming out long enough to give me an almost feverishly severe look.

"I saw it," I said again.

His chest heaved. "No," he said. And then he faded back into himself.

"You were right, all along," I said. I climbed back into my seat and closed the door. He didn't notice. "Caulder," I said, shivering, "this is not a game anymore." But I don't think he heard me, because he started to talk, almost as if he'd forgotten I was there with him.

"Why?" he murmured. "When he's never done something before in his entire life, why does he suddenly do it now? Obviously, it's got to have something to do with the movie. I mean, don't you think that's obvious? The movie, and the first one, too, then . . . something woke him up . . . something . . ."

"Caulder — " I said.

"No," he said, turning to me. "We've got to figure

62

this out. If he can cry, then he can think beyond logic and strategies. Something broke him open. He's in there — he can react emotionally. There's got to be a logical explanation — "

"Caulder," I said, staring at him, "this isn't a trig problem. This is a person. He was crying. He was *upset*."

"These were classics, right? Movie classics," he went on. "And what makes something a classic?" He made claws out of his hands and pulled at the air in front of his face. "Something that goes right to the core of human existence. It's universal. It's powerful, pure — something that connects right into the self. Right? So, if this is, like, the most powerful emotional expression we've got as a people — then it stands to reason it got through to him. It makes perfect sense."

He pulled himself upright in the seat. "Leviaton said something about that one time — what was it?" He put his palms carefully against the wheel. "He said, if it was an analysis he'd assigned — historical context, or precedence, or social impact — that kind of thing — an *objective* analysis, Tibbs could pull it off like a lawyer. But ask him for a personal reaction — any kind of value judgment or opinion, and he can't do it. He comes up with an analysis every time. It's like he has no opinions. No feelings about anything." He looked through me. "But now we know he does. It's just, he can't stand it. He can't control it. Of course, it would scare him, then, so he'd avoid it. Maybe it's that simple. Maybe that's it."

"Maybe not," I said, beginning to wish I'd just gone in the house and never said anything.

"I knew it," Caulder said, slamming his palms onto the wheel again. "I knew there was somebody in there. And we're getting somewhere — at least now we know for sure — he responds to emotion. He *feels* things."

"You can hurt somebody who's got feelings," I said, fairly sure I shouldn't have to point that out.

Caulder pursed his lips and ran his finger along a crack in the dashboard. "Okay," he said.

"Okay, what?"

"Okay. Now we really start pushing him."

"Caulder," I breathed. "What are you saying?"

He looked at me. "Whatever we're doing, it's working. We've got to keep it up."

"But what if we *hurt* him?" I asked, very clearly, so he couldn't miss the question.

Caulder looked at me. He'd just realized I was there. "Don't you get it?" he asked. "We're getting *in* there. We're waking him up. So maybe it's going to hurt him a little. Well, to save a life, maybe it's worth it. We can't think about ourselves, right now, Gin. We've got to think about what's going to be good for him . . ."

"Good for him? What's 'Best for Him,' you mean?"

"Yeah," he said. He'd totally missed my tone.

"How could *we* possibly know what's best for him?" I said, very coldly. But he didn't hear that, either.

"Look what we've done without even trying," he went on. "Now's the time for us to pay attention. We've got to push till we force him out. We've got to stop protecting him, and start treating him like he's a human being — you ask him questions, you expect an answer, you put him in normal circumstances, you interact with him — eventually, he's going to have to give himself away. Don't you understand what that means, Ginny?"

"It means we're butting into somebody else's life," I said. "It's none of our business, Caulder. We haven't been invited."

"Do you know how long I've waited just to talk to him?" Caulder asked, talking to himself again. He got out of the car. I got out, too, and we stood there with the car between us. "This is the most important thing I've ever done," he told me. "I'm going to follow it through."

He told me good night, and then he went into his house without even watching me home. Like some kind of stranger. Like somebody I didn't know at all.

My own house was dark. Nobody had remembered to leave a light on. Dark and silent, and I was all alone. I turned on the TV for a while, looking for a little comfort, but I couldn't stand that for long. So I shut it off and went to bed.

And lay there in the dark, thinking.

Smitty Tibbs with tears on his face. Smitty Tibbs could cry.

The picture made me heartsick.

What could it be like, shut up inside with everything you feel — never having the relief of expression, never sharing anything or releasing anything or trying it out on somebody else? Never asking questions? Only yourself to talk to. Only yourself to listen. Never to be understood.

Understood.

Not to be loved for what you are. Never to be known.

Tears were running down my face, now.

Smitty didn't have anybody he could trust. Not Caulder. Not the Caulder in the car with me, to-night. That Caulder wasn't Smitty's guardian angel; that Caulder was a scientist, on the verge of a great discovery — not his friend; more like his excavator. Or the mother who shunted him off to the movies to be hurt, so she could go to some meeting. Or me — a person who could be shocked to find out he was actually a human being.

If he'd been awake all this time — isolated, but hearing and seeing and feeling — what had his life meant? But then, what did anybody's life mean? Getting an education so you could get a job, so you could afford food, so you could get up in the morning and go to your job . . . feeling the things you feel, behaving the way you behave — what's the point in it all?

I lay there, staring into the dark, my heart thudding.

The front door opened.

I could hear them talking, James and Charlie — talking and laughing and shushing each other. They opened the door to my parents' room, and then they came down the hall toward mine. I closed my eyes before the light from the hall touched my face.

"I told you," whispered Charlie. And the door closed.

They went on down the hall to the kitchen and closed that door, too, so their voices were muffled, the words indistinct. I opened my eyes into the darkness and sighed. I was glad they were finally home. I hadn't realized before how much of me had been waiting for that, waiting to know they were home safe. Waiting to share the house with somebody.

"It's the family, Gin," I could hear Paul saying. *"There's nothing more important than the family."*

And maybe that's the only point there is to anything.

I remember having a fleeting interest in what James and Charlie might be eating. After that, I must have fallen asleep.

CHAPTER SIX

"You're going to be late," James yelled up from downstairs. The front door slammed. I looked at the clock and gasped. I'm only consistent when it comes to stupid things, like being late, and getting myself into awful situations. I grabbed my stuff and pulled on my jacket, flying out the front door at approximately the same moment Caulder and Smitty should have been halfway to school. But when I looked up the street, Caulder was still standing at the foot of his walk. I found this strangely disappointing.

I nodded at him, hitched my purse up on my shoulder, pulled the collar of my parka up around my ears, and stood at the foot of my walk, waiting and catching my breath. I guess it didn't occur to me to go over and wait with Caulder. I just stood there at the end of my walk with my books in my arms, breathing little clouds out into the air.

After a minute, Caulder came trudging over to me.

"Aren't we late?" I asked him. He shrugged, peered at Tibbs's house, scowled at his watch, and took another look at the house.

"Maybe he's sick," Caulder said, sounding worried. *Well, that's good of you,* I thought.

"Maybe he hates our guts," I said.

"There is that," he allowed. Reluctantly, he started down the sidewalk toward school.

"You could go check," I suggested. Caulder turned around and took one more look at the Tibbses'. "No," he said, finally. "We're late enough as it is." He started walking again.

"I thought you were worried," I said, following him down the sidewalk.

"Well," he retorted. "*You* want to go over there? Mrs. Tibbs is probably still in her robe — you could see what her hair looks like in the morning — "

"No thanks," I said. So we went on to school, neither of us saying a word.

As it turned out, Smitty wasn't sick. He was sitting in homeroom. He didn't bat an eyelash when I caught it for coming in after the bell. And I was angry about that — mad that we'd stood there in the freezing cold, waiting for him. Mad that I'd caught heck in front of the whole class — that it was his fault, and I was never going to get any satisfaction out of knowing he knew it.

He was getting more human every minute.

It was hours before I finally realized that Smitty had been making another statement. Of course, even a halfway intelligent dog would act to avoid an uncomfortable situation, but still — it was like an affirmation of our very existence, that he shouldn't want to walk with us.

If that's why he hadn't shown up this morning.

"Well, I think we can assume he definitely is avoiding us," Caulder said that night. We were on

69

our way home from the Tibbses' with my math. Smitty hadn't helped me; his mother hadn't been able to find him anywhere.

"You'd better be able to explain this stuff to me, Caulder," I warned him, meaning my math. "This is your fault."

He glared at me. "Oh, really," he said.

"Yes, really," I told him. We turned in at my walk. "I have to hand in this stuff tomorrow, Caulder. The way my luck is running, Mrs. Shein will probably ask me to explain it at the board."

"Which you could do, if you wanted to," he said. "If you'd stop whining and use half your brain."

"Which I could do, if I had anybody who could explain it to me. Which I would have if we'd just left Smitty alone in the first place."

"Oh. *Now* it comes out. She cares more about getting her grade in math than she does about helping another human being."

"Oh. *Helping.*"

"Yes. Helping." Caulder had his nose stuck up in the air.

"You're a real truck driver, you know that, Caulder? As long as you get where you think you're going, you don't care who you make into roadkill."

He turned around and stared at me. "And what's that supposed to mean?"

"You think you're Albert Schweitzer or somebody, but you're not. You'd probably cut down rain forests and call it 'Progress for Mankind.' "

He narrowed his eyes at me. "You've been weird all day," he said to me. "So, what's the problem?"

"The problem is, you don't really care about Smitty."

His mouth fell open. "How can you say that to me? What do you mean, I don't care about him? What do you want me to do? Die for him or something? I love him, you know I love him."

I folded my arms and took a breath. And then I looked him square in the face. "You don't hurt people you love."

His hands fell down at his sides. He looked away from me, and then he took a breath and he met my eyes. "You do if you have to." He lifted his hands slightly and then dropped them. "I don't want to hurt him," he said. "God knows I don't."

We were standing on my front stoop, freezing, staring each other down.

"You do what you have to do," he said, softly.

"What you *have* to do," I echoed.

"You do your best," he amended. Then he sighed and leaned back against the wall of my house. "Sometimes I get carried away," he admitted. "But — " he looked up at me " — I think maybe sometimes you run when it looks like it's going to cost you anything."

A little tongue of anger flared up inside of me at that, not so much because he was criticizing me, but because I suspected he was right. "This isn't about me," I said.

"This is about us," he finished wearily. "And maybe why we need each other. And maybe why he needs both of us, and not just me."

I still had my arms folded, but something in all that had sounded like reconciliation and, suddenly, I wasn't angry with Caulder anymore.

"What about my math?" I said.

I saw him relax. "Don't worry about your math,"

he said, making it sound dogged. "I'm not as useless as I make out."

Which turned out to be a good thing, as Caulder was the only help I was going to be getting for days to come.

No Smitty in the morning, no Smitty at night. No matter how Caulder lay in wait, Smitty out-guessed us, and I got yelled at more than once for being late to homeroom. The one time Smitty was late, the teacher didn't say a word to him. Caulder was right: That kid had a very good thing going, in some ways.

The one bright spot in my life that week was *supposed* to have been the film society. They were showing *Mr. Smith Goes to Washington*, a movie I actually *knew* something about. A happy film — actually funny in places. Exactly the thing I needed. James and Charlie and the girls had bailed out early in the week, having something *far* more meaningful to do on Friday. But that was okay; it meant Caulder and I could be old people, alone together — old, tired people who sorely needed a tandem sense of emotional satisfaction. It was going to be restorative. It was going to be lovely. This is what I sincerely believed.

Then Thursday night, Caulder gave me this triumphant look and announced that he had *finally* asked Hally out. And where was he planning to take her? Any guesses? To the film society, of course. To *Mr. Smith Goes to Washington*.

And I was supposed to be pleased. I was supposed to be *proud* of him.

When it finally got through to him that I wasn't, he was offended. "Was this not what you wanted?

Did you not persecute me into doing this?" he demanded, and then, turning to everyone else, "Did she not?"

"She did," they all intoned solemnly.

"Then why is she looking at me like that?"

There was a moment of silence.

"What is *she* going to do Friday night?" I asked him. "While you and your *girlfriend* are going to *our* movie?"

"Well, you can come, too," he said, very simply.

"*Right*," I said. Kaitlin and Melissa agreed with me.

"What?" he said again. "Why not?"

"He is *so* stupid," I said to his sisters.

"Caulder," Kaitlin said, very patiently. "You can't ask one girl out and have another girl tag along."

"I thought this was an enlightened age," Caulder protested.

"You can't ask one girl out and have another girl tag along," Kaitlin repeated, "no matter what age it is."

"Hally wants to go out with *you*, not with *us*," I pointed out.

"But she's *your* friend," he said. And then, with sudden comprehension, "She *wants* to go out with me?"

"You are so *stupid*," I said again. "You are so — *typical*." I got up from the table. "I'm going for a walk," I said. "I'm glad you asked Hally out — okay? I'm really glad. Glad for you, glad for Hally, glad you all have someplace to go Friday night. I hope you all have a *great* time." I couldn't help the look I gave him, and I got my coat, and I went outside.

"Just leave her alone, Mr. Sensitive," I heard Kaitlin say as I pulled on my coat. "She'll take care of herself."

I slammed the front door and stood there steaming in the dark, chill October night. I stalked down the walk and started down the ground — going nowhere, really, just giving Caulder and the whole rest of the world a good, mental pounding.

I walked two blocks and gave up. *So, what about me?* I was thinking. I stopped and sat in the gutter. *Everybody else in the world gets what they want. Oh, of course, they love me. I'm great to have around as long as you don't have anything better to do. Paul takes off for college, my folks drag us out here and then desert us, the kids take off with their friends, Caulder deserts me — it's not even because he's so stupid. It's not even because he's mean. It's because I'm the kind of person people forget, that's why. I just might as well not even exist. I'm not the kind of person people fight for. I'm just sort of an extra. I might as well just sit here the rest of my life. Alone. In the gutter.*

The wind blew and a smattering of leaves hit the street, scudding away from me. I looked up. There wasn't another soul in the street. There were lights in the windows of the houses, but they seemed cold and distant. There were no cars moving. Only the wind. I could have been the only person alive in the whole world. And that's the way I felt. It was very depressing. I picked up a little chip of broken asphalt and balanced it on my palm.

"This is stupid," I said out loud. I chucked the asphalt into the street. I was still too mad to give in to depression. So I got up and walked back down the street toward my house. *Okay,* I said to myself, quoting Paul, *what is it, exactly, Ginny, that you want?* At the moment, that was easy to answer. I wanted to see that stupid movie. *So go alone.* Of course. Walk ten blocks in the dark and freeze to death on the way. *So go with them.* Unthinkable. *Pride getting in your way?* Maybe so. I'm just funny that way.

I stopped in the middle of the sidewalk, frustrated and angry and fed up with myself. I looked up and found myself glaring at the pale-blue rectangles of the Tibbses' living room windows.

"People allow themselves to be defeated," Paul told me one time. *"Like that time I fell off the horse? I didn't have to fall off it. There was actually a moment — just this one, silvery little moment — when it could have gone either way."* He'd opened his hands. *"I gave up. My choice was to let go. So, I ended up with my face in the dirt and a concussion. Of course, if I'd stayed on, I'd probably have broken my neck . . ."*

"Okay," I said to myself, and without any clear idea of what I was going to do, I marched up the walk and knocked on the door.

Mrs. Tibbs looked a little surprised to see me. Alone, that is — without Caulder. She stood there at the door, smiling politely, waiting.

"Would you tell Smitty I'm here?" I asked her. "Could you tell him I'm here by myself, and I need to talk to him?"

She was obviously too polite to shut the door in my face. After a moment, she stepped back and let me in. Her brows were all delicately puckered. "Where's Caulder?" she asked me, peering out over my shoulder into the dark as though she thought he'd suddenly pop up there.

"I believe he's studying," I said.

She sighed, but she finally showed me into the living room, putting out a hand to indicate that she expected me to perch myself on her brocade sofa.

"And you want to see Smitty about . . . ?" she asked. I could hear a TV on in the back of the house.

"It's kind of private," I said. I said it apologetically. "I just need to talk to Smitty. I won't upset him." Actually, I was lying. I didn't care if I *did* upset him.

She laughed this tiny, half-exasperated laugh. "I think you can imagine how strange I find all this," she said.

I smiled at her. I didn't know what else to do. By this time, I was pretty sure she was going to tell me to go home and leave her family alone.

"Well," she said, a little helplessly. "I guess I'll get him for you."

When she left, I was so relieved, I almost forgot myself and relaxed against the back of that sofa, but then I started thinking about how embarrassing it was going to be when she came down and told me he wouldn't come. I straightened up, trying for a little dignity. That room was not exactly exuding hospitality — it looked like some kind of museum exhibit, perfect and frozen in eternity. The piano was so polished, you could have seen the fingerprints a mile away — if anybody'd ever touched it. The only human things in there were the piled up newspapers in the corner, and the little picture of Smitty and his brother and his parents that sat in a gilt frame on the piano.

Smitty came into the room.

What had made him decide he could finally come down, I couldn't guess. His mother stood in the doorway behind him. "I'll be in the den," she said, watching him until he sat down. Then she left us alone. Smitty picked up a *National Geographic* off an end table and opened it.

"I'm here because I need to take charge of my life," I started. The sound of my voice hung in the air for a moment before it got sucked up by the blue carpet and the sheer blue drapes.

"I need somebody to talk to, and I can't talk to my mother, because she's working with my dad, and I can't talk to my older brother, Paul, because he's at college, and I can't talk to Hally because she's part of the problem, and I can't talk to Caulder because he's the other part, and the rest of my family is over there with a bunch of friends *and* Caulder, which makes it so I can't talk to *any*body. So, I have chosen to talk to *you*. And if you don't like it, I'm sorry. And if you don't hear me, that's fine. Just so you sit there and try to remember you're a fellow human being."

He just sat there.

"I have to admit," I said bitterly, "that right now, I'm feeling very sorry for myself. It seems like everybody in the world but me has somebody who cares about them. Like I'm good company as long as nothing better comes along. Caulder is my best friend. But now Caulder is taking Hally out on Friday — which is the night Caulder and I *always* do something together" — I blushed a little, here — "as you already know. So, the upshot is, this Friday night, *I* get to sit home alone, without anybody. Reading a book or something, which is not *my* idea of a bang-up Friday night, if you have any life at all. Which I don't. Unless it's convenient for somebody else to remember that I happen to be there.

"I swear, something's *wrong* with me, or why doesn't somebody ask me out? People *used* to ask me out. But these people probably think I don't *want* to go out. They probably think I *want* to spend every night with Caulder. And now Caulder's got a date and *you're* no use at all. It's not like *you're* going to ask me out. And even if you did, I'd probably just end up doing something offensive, and you'd stalk off and leave me feeling like a fool. So, where am I after all this? All by myself on Friday night, that's where.

"Well, I don't want to be by myself. I want to see *Mr. Smith Goes to Washington*, which is the movie this Friday, and which I happen to know for a fact is sweet and wonderful and all about the triumph of personal honor, and not about anything terrible, except, maybe, politics. But here's the thing: I can't go unless *you* go, because — *a*, I can't go with Caulder unless we double, and *b*, I certainly can't go alone. So I'm asking you — *please*, whatever it is we did to you that was so terrible — which we did *not* mean to do — *forgive* us, and come with me, so I don't have to sit home all by myself, which I really, really, *really* don't want to do."

At least I had dignity enough not to let any tears actually spill over. I stood up with great dignity. "I'll be in that car with them tomorrow night, and we'll come down here at seven-fifteen, and we'll honk. If you want to come, you come. If you don't, I'll just get out of the car and go home. Otherwise, I'm paying for the tickets, because I'm the one asking you out. That's all I have to say. I hope you can hear me. Thank you for coming down."

And then I left.

I walked up and down the sidewalk some more, feeling humiliated, and wondering how I was going to tell Caulder what I'd done.

Everybody looked up when I came in. I just stood there, daring them to say anything. "I may have a date for the movie, myself, tomorrow night," I announced, leaving no space for comment and definitely looking like I wouldn't welcome any. "And now, I would like it very much if you would explain my math to me."

Caulder gave me no argument.

But it must have killed him, wondering where I'd been.

CHAPTER SEVEN

Caulder is so nervous, he could die — don't tell him I told you. I was starting my morning howdy-to-Hally note in homeroom. *By the way, we're doubling, sort of. Maybe. I know that wasn't what you expected. I hope you don't hate me.*

Nifty, nifty, she wrote back. *Who with? Petey-baby?*

Mrs. Eagle Eye was not fond of note-passers. We had made an art out of getting a note from my desk to Hally's without having it snagged.

Smitty Tibbs. I was in agony, watching Hally as she read it, hoping she wouldn't freak or laugh or, worse, be totally repulsed. I guess I shouldn't have worried. But she did look surprised.

"So," she said, once we were out of class and free to breathe, "how did this come about?"

I shrugged. "Caulder and I have kind of made a tradition of going to the film society on Friday nights, and sometimes we take Smitty with us."

"Oh," she said, slowing down right in the middle of the hall. She stopped and looked at me, square on. "Tell the truth — is this messing you up? Me coming along, tonight?" I could have kicked myself for having made it sound that way.

"*No,*" I lied, and then followed with a quick truth — "I'm just worried I'm messing things up for *you.*"

"Don't worry about it," she said, cheerfully shrugging us back into the mainstream of traffic. "I hate first dates, anyway." We walked along in companionable silence for a while, and then she said, "Smitty is still a little spooky to me. Which isn't to say that I don't respect him as a person." She looked at me. "What's it like? Going places with him?"

"Kind of strange," I said.

"That's what I thought. Well, I guess I'll find out, huh?"

If things work out, tonight, I thought.

I was nervous the rest of the day, and unsettled. I hate it when you don't know what's going to happen — when you're not even sure how you feel about what's going to happen — it's like, you have to be prepared to handle every possible scenario. It's not possible to be that well-adjusted.

As it turned out, Caulder and Hally picked me up, we all drove over to Smitty's house, and there was Smitty, standing at the end of his walk. Caulder got out and opened the car door for him, and Smitty got into the backseat with me.

That's all there was to it.

Caulder pulled away from the curb, Hally chatting along cheerfully in the front seat. She even managed to get the nerve-stricken Caulder's verbal motor running, and their talk began to fill up the inside of the car. For a while, I felt like I should be helping them break the ice — until I finally realized there was no ice up there that needed breaking. Then I sat back into my own seat, maybe a little embarrassed, glancing sidelong at Smitty.

All day, I'd been a little appalled at what I'd done

— not because I'd gone over to Smitty's and asked him to come, because I don't see what's wrong with that, socially. I mean, it's embarrassing and all, but it's no worse than what guys go through all the time. It was *who* I'd asked out. When I could have chosen anybody. It made me feel a little bit strange about myself.

Smitty had found himself a comfortable place on the seat, his head back, his eyes half-closed. I kind of snugged myself over into the far corner of the seat, dropped my hands into my lap, and sighed.

Hally and Caulder were laughing about something. I sighed again. Gradually, the sound of their voices dropped a blanket of peaceful detachment across the two of us in the back. We were just going where they were taking us, no responsibility in the matter at all. I began to relax. *This must be what it's like for Smitty*, I realized — *going where they take you, but thinking your own thoughts.*

We parked in the usual place, walked up the hill, and waited in line, the three of us joking around together, but once we got into the auditorium, I caught at the slack on Smitty's sleeve, effectively stopping him, and waited for Caulder and Hally to go on down the aisle a ways without us. They didn't even notice we were gone.

"They need to be alone," I explained to Smitty, feeling a little like I was explaining things to Lassie. "So, why don't we sit back here?"

He didn't move a muscle, just stood there in his usual suspended state, until I finally understood I was in charge of deciding where to sit. So I found us a couple of seats, led the way, and we sat down. Ginny and Smitty, alone together.

How I was going to keep up a one-sided conversation, I didn't know. But as we sat there waiting for the lights to go off, I realized that I didn't have to talk. Smitty didn't require that. He just sat, so I just sat, looking around, thinking. And it wasn't bad. I sighed, and slid down into the seat.

Then the movie started. It was great — you got to root for right and truth and innocence and, in the end, virtue and love came through triumphant, just the way they always should and hardly ever seem to. And when the lights came up, Smitty was still sitting there. I felt the best I had in a long, long time — at peace with the world, knowing God's in his Heaven, believing in True Love, the Triumph of Simple Goodness, and the Ultimate Unity of Mankind, and thinking it might actually be possible for things to turn out all right in the end.

I waited until Caulder and Hally came by, and then we filed out after them, up the hall, down the stairs, and out into the night air. I let the other two get a little ahead, allowing them their privacy. It was velvet dark as soon as we got down over the edge of campus, out of so many lights and under the trees. And it was cold. I shoved my hands deep into the pockets of my parka, nestled my chin down into the collar, and blew out a tiny, contented cloud of mist.

Hally and Caulder passed under a streetlight ahead of us. They were holding hands. I got a little shock, looking at that little heart-shaped knot their

hands were making. They were connected now —
no longer through me. And they were making a
new place between them with every step they took
and every word they said to each other. Suddenly,
I was feeling very outside, and very much colder.

I glanced at Smitty's empty, serene face.

I wondered if his coming tonight had actually
had anything to do with me. Maybe he'd forgotten
abut last week already. Maybe he hadn't even been
waiting for us — maybe he'd just been standing
there at the end of his walk, minding his own
business, and we just sort of kidnapped him.

But I didn't believe any of that. I knew he'd come
with us tonight because I'd asked him to come. And
he'd been taking a chance, doing it. That seemed
like kindness to me. I had a fleeting impression,
then, of a personality in the body walking beside
me. I looked up at him shyly and smiled. But he
didn't see.

Hally and Caulder were waiting for us at the
car. Caulder was grinning, and he wouldn't look
me straight in the eye. Hally was a little flushed
in the face.

"My brother and I decided to have a little before-
Halloween party next week," Hally told us as we
climbed into the car and started fishing for seat
belts. "You want to come? All you guys? You, too,
Smitty. All you guys come together. You come and
be my man, okay, Caulder?" she said, just as cute
as you please — utterly captivating, judging by
the look on Caulder's face.

"Great," I said.

Caulder was really feeling good. He backed that
car right out of its parking place like a man in

charge of his own destiny. "Let's take a ride," he said, expansively. "It's not really that late."

And so we did. Caulder and Hally went about setting up their quiet wall of conversation, and Smitty settled back into his seat, looking very comfortable and almost sleepy.

I was snuggled down into my corner again, watching him as the streetlights flickered across the backseat.

Caulder headed out toward the country where the roads were smooth and long.

Smitty's eyes were closed. The car was warm, and the dark drone of the tires against the road was peaceful, almost hypnotic. Smitty opened his eyes, and laid his head back against the seat, watching the darkness go by outside. I could see his face reflected in his window, planes of light and shadow, and eyes that were dark pools.

The face I saw there was harsh and empty, but looking at it made me realize what a gentle face Smitty actually had, and it seemed to me then that the person behind it must also be gentle — a gentle, quiet heart, tucked away from what could be a hard, stupid world. I wondered if it was sweet where he was, or if he was lonely in there. And at that moment, inside my soul, I moved over next to him, put my arm through his and rested my head on his shoulder.

I sat up straight and turned my face to the window. My breath clouded it immediately, and I couldn't see anything but the mist I'd made. My heart was pounding in my ears. *What were you thinking?* I rested my forehead against the window. My hands were shaking.

And then I told myself — *of course, you could never do such a thing.* I was trying to look at the whole thing very rationally. I sat up in the seat and folded my hands in my lap. I could imagine what might have happened to him if I'd touched him then, trapped in the backseat of this car the way he was. A nightmare. A nightmare. And me. I was suddenly scared. And shocked. It hadn't been pity I'd been imagining just then, the nice, normal girl having compassion on the poor, mentally damaged person. No. The thing I had felt was something completely different than that, something deep and totally inappropriate for a girl like me to have for a person like him. Something that now had me suddenly terrified about my own sanity.

Maybe it was just that I was lonelier than I'd ever guessed. I turned to the window again. The mist was gone. The stars were clear and sharp out here, away from the glow of the town lights. After a minute, I worked up my courage and looked over at Smitty again. He hadn't moved. He was just sitting there, watching the stars, all unaware of me. *And what are you thinking? Where in the name of heaven are you?*

Suddenly, I knew how lonely I was. Lost.

"I loved that movie," I whispered, not necessarily to be heard. "I love happy endings. Paul and I used to make popcorn and sit around in our pajamas, watching that old black and white stuff on channel two. Me and my brother, Paul. We always liked the ones that ended like that." I felt tears in my eyes and I turned back to the stars.

When I looked at Smitty again, his eyes were closed, his hands folded, asleep for all I knew.

86

So, I started talking. It was kind of strange, but everything that had been sitting so heavily in my heart seemed to be coming out of me, all in a whisper, here in the backseat of Caulder's mother's car. I talked about all my brothers, about the way it used to be when we were all together. I talked about the old house and Christmases past, about how I missed Paul, and about how there hadn't been any family since we'd left home, how it was all changing, and would never be the same again — how it was all going to keep unravelling until there was nothing left at all —

I began to feel drowsy after a while, the way I used to feel when I was little, riding along, half-asleep in the back of the car at night, coming home from Nana's. Floating, kind of — distant and detached. I could hear my own voice, as though it were somebody else's.

And Smitty sat low in the seat, his head back and his eyes closed, maybe asleep — but maybe there, maybe hearing.

I owe you. Hally wrote to me on Monday. *You name it, you can have it. Caulder is great. Caulder is wonderful. I got my brother to invite Pete's brother to my party, and — by the way — he's supposed to bring Pete. Just for you. So there. We'll be even.*

It was like she'd stuck ammonia or something under my nose, the jolt I got from that note — pure terror. But, hey — this was adventure, right? And it was a shoo-in that nothing would ever come of it. So I dusted off my sense of humor, pulled a piece of paper out of my notebook, and I wrote *You really invited Pete? This is Peter Zabriski, we're talking* about? *Gorgeous Peter Zabriski?????? He won't come. I'm not even sure I want him to come. What would I say to him? You think he'll bring his French horn? Ah, sweet mystery of life, I've found you.* I even drew little hearts over all the little *i*'s.

I folded it up, watched for my chance, and tossed it over to Hally's desk.

I never dreamed the teacher would get that one.

Not only did she intercept it — she read it. Out loud. In front of the *entire class.*

"I believe this is yours, Ms. Christianson?" the woman said, just in case anybody should not have had a completely clear idea who it was being publicly executed.

This kind of thing doesn't die an easy death. By first lunch, every human being in that school knew I had a crush on Pete Zabriski. That was just all I needed.

"Do *not* invite him to that party," I told Hally after class. "Because if you do, I'm not coming."

"You got it," she said. Made no difference to her. "By the way, Smitty Tibbs was looking at you today."

"Oh, yeah?" That gave me a little jolt, too.

"Well, as much as he ever looks at anything. It was more like he was looking through you, but yes — his eyes were definitely focused somewhere over your left shoulder. It was toward the end of class. It's not like you would have noticed. You weren't doing a lot of looking around today."

That was an understatement.

"Well, you gotta stop passing notes," Caulder said to me when he and his sisters came over to study with us that night. He was grinning his head off.

"Shut up," I told him. I put my nose in the air, and picked up my world history text so he'd know I wasn't interested in discussing it. "Who told you?" I asked from behind the book.

"Who didn't?" he said, cheerfully.

I slammed the book closed and pressed the cover against my face. "I'm not ever going back there," I said.

"Come on," he said.

"I'm not." I slammed the book down onto my knees. "I *hate* stuff like this."

"Stuff like what?" James asked, glancing up from his English.

"Like, public humiliation."

"She got caught passing notes this morning," Caulder said.

"Oh, yeah?" James said, interested.

"Was it awful?" Kaitlin asked, looking very sympathetic.

"The note was all about Pete Zabriski and how *cute* he is," Caulder said. "And Mrs. Attila the Hun read it out loud."

"Did you die?" Kaitlin asked. From my face, she got her answer.

"I think it's romantic," Melissa said. "He'll probably ask you out now. He probably didn't know you were interested in him before."

"I'm not that interested in him," I said, but I had to admit — it would have been nice to dance with him just once at Hally's party. No chance of that, now.

"I am never," I said solemnly, "*ever* going to step outside of this house ever, ever again."

"She's just tired," Caulder told them. "Come on, you," he said to me, pulling me up by the back of my sweater, "let's take a walk." He made me put on my coat, and then he made me go outside.

"It's cold out there," I protested. Well — whined, actually.

He put his arm around my shoulders and steered me down the front walk. "Now, now," he said, using his most patronizing male voice and patting me on the head. "Nice girls like you just seem to get less dates than the other kind do. You mustn't let this bother you. Some day, the right man will come along . . ."

I hit him with my elbow. "Funny."

He let me go. "Well, what do you expect? Writing that kind of thing about Zabriski. You should have written something nice about me. Then nobody would have been surprised."

I sighed. "Is there some reason we have to be out here in the freezing cold?" I asked him. "I mean, besides the fact that I swore I'd never come out of my house again?"

He didn't answer for a moment. Then he said, "I told my mother about the other night. That you saw Smitty crying. I told her not to say anything to Mrs. Tibbs about it, but she probably will, anyway."

"Oh, Caulder," I said.

"I know. But it's good I did it. Because she told me something I didn't know before."

I breathed on my hands and waited.

"There was one other time he cried."

"I thought you told me he never had," I said.

"Well, like I say, I didn't know." He turned us around back toward my house. "It happened about five years ago when Russell was still living at home."

"Who's Russell?"

"Smitty's brother."

"Oh, yeah," I said. "I asked you about him, before. How come I never see him?"

"He's been away at school for the past couple of years. He's getting married this Christmas. My mom's supposed to help with the flowers. She's not real happy about it."

"How come?"

"Well — she doesn't really like Russell very much." He was going to say something else, but he pulled his mouth closed.

"Why not?" I asked, prodding him with my elbow.

"Well, because. . . ." He sighed. "Russell's not . . . well — I don't really like him very much, either."

"Why? He beat you up when you were little?" I teased.

Caulder glanced at me and grinned. "Not me. I never got in his way." He hunched his shoulders against the cold. "You know how Mrs. Tibbs is about community service? Well, she's always been like that. When Smitty was little, she would leave him with Russell, but Russell was always more or less on his own. So he's always done pretty much whatever he wanted. Like once, Carmen Anders, that woman who lives in the yellow house down at the end of the street? Carmen yelled at Russell

91

for running across her flower beds. Two days later, somebody threw a rock through her front window. A week later, her cat disappeared."

"Come on," I said.

"Nobody could ever prove anything. Russell used to get away with murder. See, Russell used to have two kinds of effects on people — either they didn't like him, and they could see right through him, or else they really bought his act — because, see, he could be sweet as anything when he wanted to be. His mother always bought it. I, myself, always thought it was wiser to stay out of his way altogether."

"Didn't anybody ever complain to his parents?"

Caulder laughed. "Sure, they did," he said. "And Mr. Tibbs was always willing to pay for the damage or whatever, but Mrs. Tibbs always complained to my mother about it afterward. She'd say 'I *know* Russell didn't do it. He would *never* do anything like that. Sometimes I wonder if John really *loves* Russell. He's so hard on him.' And then she'd talk about how 'boys will be boys' and how intolerant she thought the neighbors were. My mom really doesn't like Mrs. Tibbs very much, either. But don't *ever* tell anybody I said that."

"So, what's he like, now?"

He lifted one shoulder. "Who knows? Maybe he's grown up. Maybe not."

"Why didn't his dad just wale on him?" I said, disgusted. "My parents would never take stuff like that from us. If it was even *hinted* I'd done something wrong, they'd be on me like velcro on a shoelace."

Caulder looked thoughtful. "I think Mr. Tibbs tried — at least, at first. The Tibbs used to fight about it a lot — I could hear them from my bedroom window sometimes. But then they stopped. Now, Mr. Tibbs hardly ever says a word. I mean, once in a while he'll say 'hi' to my dad over the back fence. But when he's home he's usually hanging around this shop he's got back in the garage — he restores antique cars. Other than that, he just kind of keeps to himself."

"Nice family," I said.

"They're okay neighbors," Caulder said. "They could be worse. Anyway, Mrs. Tibbs asked my mom to do the flowers for the wedding, and my mom couldn't tell her no."

"You were going to tell me a story," I reminded him.

"I was? Oh, yeah, I was. Okay, so, about five years ago, Russell got into archery. He had this target set up in the backyard, and the neighbors — including my mother — were always yelling at the Tibbs because they were afraid Russell was going to end up killing somebody. Or shooting somebody in the eye with an arrow, or something. So finally, his dad went out there and took the target down, and told Russell he was going to have to go to the country if he wanted to shoot.

"So, this one day, Russell comes home — from shooting in the country — he comes home and he's all proud of himself because he'd shot a bird. You know — like, on the wing, which is not easy. Probably illegal, but not easy. So, he's in the kitchen, telling his mother about it — and this is the strange part — Smitty's just sitting there, and suddenly he gets up and he goes over to Russell and he throws this glass of orange juice right in

Russell's face. I mean, *right* in his face."

"*Smitty* did?" I said, just making sure I'd heard right.

"I know. It's weird. Maybe he was upset about the bird —"

"Which you could hardly blame him for." Personally, I think people who kill things for pleasure are sick.

"Or, maybe not — who knows what's going on in his mind? Anyway, Russell got up and knocked Smitty halfway across the room. Knocked him out, totally."

I stopped. "Knocked him out?" I echoed.

"Yeah. Come on. We're going to freeze if we just stand here. They had to take Smitty to emergency, and they ended up having to leave him overnight because they couldn't wake him up. So it was in the middle of the night, this nurse went in to check him, and Smitty was crying in his sleep."

The pain in my chest caught me a little bit by surprise.

"She still couldn't wake him up, so she called the doctor, and got the family history from him. As it turns out, she was a student at the university med school, in psychology and counseling, and she ended up getting real interested in Smitty. The next day, she asked the Tibbs if she could work with him. Of course, they thought that was a great idea. But then something happened, like her father died, or something, and she had to go away for a while. Then she had to go and do her specialization and internship somewhere.

"When she came back here a couple of years ago to work at the university clinic, she was still interested, but they couldn't get Smitty to go for it. I mean, it's not like he actually objected or anything — you know the way he disappears. Every couple of months, now, she calls. It never works out. Mrs. Tibbs called *her* last week — I guess she was thinking, since he's been letting us come over, maybe he'd go for it this time. But he faded on her, again. Anyway, the psychologist wants us to keep coming around."

I looked at him. This scared me.

"I know," he said. "It makes me feel weird, too."

"And now your mother will tell Mrs. Tibbs about the other night . . ."

"And then Mrs. Tibbs'll tell the psychologist," he finished.

"I don't like this at all," I said, feeling this awful pressure in my chest. "I feel like Judas."

"I know," he said.

We stood there huddled together in the cold.

"Let's not go to the Tibbses' tonight," I said, shivering. "He never asked for any of this. We've just done it to him. And then we go over there and ask him for help."

"No, I think we ought to go," Caulder said. "It's up to him to decide if he wants to help us or not. If he didn't want us to come, he'd let us know. I think he wants us there."

So we tucked up our guilt, and we went. And it was business as usual — me confused, Smitty patiently going over the problems, time after time, every step spelled out so a kindergartner could understand it.

It was nice that one of us should understand something.

CHAPTER EIGHT

Pete Zabriski — who had never, not for the tiniest fraction of a moment, ever been *remotely* aware that I existed — *smiled* at me during lunch.

It was so embarrassing, I dropped my spoon.

"What?" Caulder said. We'd been sharing his tapioca. I just looked at him. *"What?"* he asked again.

"A person should be able to do her chewing and swallowing secure from the risk of humiliation," I said.

"Pardon me?" he said.

"I've got some studying to do." I stood up.

"What? *Now?*" Caulder said. "It's *lunch.*"

"Yes, now," I said, and I left him sitting there all by himself with the rest of the tapioca. I had a sudden horror of finding myself in an unstructured environment with a person like Pete Zabriski who obviously knew how to capitalize on a person's discomfort. No more first lunch. Not for now. Maybe never again.

The only alternative was to switch lunches, at least temporarily. It would take some finagling, but I have always found inconvenience more than slightly preferable to terminal humiliation. Of course, as it turned out, it would have been *much* better if I'd just toughed it out and left things as they were.

Just after third period next day, Caulder passed me in the hall and stuffed a wad of papers on top of the books I was carrying, waggling his eyebrows and grinning like he was really satisfied with himself.

When I got to Mrs. Shein's room, I put the books down on the floor and spread Caulder's wad out flat on the desk. It turned out to be a long report, folded into loose quarters, as if somebody'd meant to throw it away. The title read: A Partial Analysis of Bismark's Application of Selected Machiavellian Principles by Michael S. Tibbs.

So this was one of Smitty's papers.

I riffled through the pages — ten pages long with footnotes on every page. For Leviaton's class. Leviaton hadn't assigned any research so far this year. So, this was Smitty's idea of what you did for a regular assignment. Top of the class? I guess so.

I'd read as far as the third page when the bell rang. It was impressive; he wrote like an adult, with a sentence structure that was definitely more complex than anything I could have done. Actually, it read like a well-written textbook — clear, but without much life in it. No personality. It was actually more or less exactly what you'd have expected.

Mrs. Shein had started going over the last night's assignment.

I leafed through the rest of the paper while I reached down for my notebook. I hauled the notebook up onto my desk, flipped it open to the math section, and blew Smitty's report off the desk. I bent over to retrieve the report, and when I straightened up with it, a little piece of paper fluttered from between the pages. I shoved the rest of Smitty's paper into my notebook, and then I reached down again for that little scrap. I could see that there was writing all over it, as though it were a note of some kind, which was curious. I wanted to read it right then, but when I straightened up again, I finally noticed that everybody was watching me.

"Are you quite finished?" Mrs. Shein asked — not unkindly.

My cheeks went hot, and I nodded. She smiled. I leaned over to get my math book, which I deposited, unopened, on my desk, and then leaned over again to stick the little scrap from Smitty's paper into my purse.

"You weren't finished," Mrs. Shein observed.

"I am now," I said. She smiled. I wanted to put my head down on the desk.

That feeling was destined to last way past lunch.

I spent first lunch hiding out in the library — which was legal, as long as you didn't bring in food. I buried myself back in the reference section, away from the slings and arrows of social ridicule, spread out my books, and started digging around in my purse for my pen. When I finally unearthed it, there was that mysterious little scrap from Smitty's paper, wrapped neatly around it. I'd nearly forgotten about it.

I still thought it was a note. As I peeled the bit of paper off the pen, I pretty well decided it couldn't have been Smitty's; who was going to be passing notes with Smitty Tibbs? Then, when I could see the writing more clearly, the regularity of the lines made me think it was probably just the rough notes he'd made for his paper.

But as I began to read, the planet slipped quietly on its axis; the truth of the matter was as far from my conjecture as Beta Centauri is from Chicago. This was not a note of any kind. It was a poem.

I read the first line and stopped.

Poetry is not my best thing. T.S. Eliot, I never understand — Edger A. Guest and his clones, I understand all too easily. I land somewhere to the obscure left of middle — e.e. cummings, I like. And Gerard Manley Hopkins, who I also never understand, but whose words make music inside me.

This poem was like that, like Hopkins. At least, the first line was.

I read the first line again, and then I read it still again, out loud this time, whispering. I went on through all the lines, going slowly, carefully, because the meaning wasn't at all concrete.

The images were full of flight. Lights lanced through them, glancing off edges that might have been the tips of wings — and there was air, like the headiness of freedom, like an independence from the bounds of earth — exactly the opposite of darkness. It was an incredible thing to read.

I finally stopped and put my hand down on top of the paper, my eyes closed against those pictures.

What was this doing in Smitty's paper? And how had Caulder gotten ahold of it?

I read it through one more time, my hands pressed together, the tips of them at my lips.

The fact that this had been stuck inside Smitty's paper was uncontestable — you could see the fold lines on it. The question had more to do with how it had gotten there. I picked up the scrap, squinted at the writing, trying to see some element of Smitty's math proof printing on it. If I'd known for certain the writing was Smitty's, that would have told me something — or maybe not; obviously, he'd copied it down for a reason, maybe for another paper . . . but maybe not. Maybe he'd just copied it because he'd liked it. I thought about that for a moment, and felt my heart speeding up.

If Smitty Tibbs read poetry — if he *liked* it. . . .

I looked down at the little piece of paper in my hands. If he had written this down the same way I do, he'd done it to make the words his own, because these words had spoken something he couldn't have said himself. And if that was so, what I had in my hand was an open window into somebody else's house.

I put the poem down on the table in front of me.

I was trespassing.

The interim bell rang. I swallowed, picked up the little paper, and slipped it into the pocket of my shirt. Then I gathered up my things and went to meet Hally.

She was waiting for me by the cafeteria door. "I'm so glad you deserted Caulder," she said. "I never could figure out why you guys feel like you've got to eat so early."

For a millisecond, I considered showing her the poem. She was the only other person I knew — except, maybe, Charlie — who would be able to hear the spaces and the speed and the release of passion that I felt in it. And she would probably know where it had come from, what age of sudden, wild vision. But I found I didn't want to show it to her. I didn't even want to sit around and chat, just then. I had this quiet feeling inside of me, the way you do when you've been in a church or something. Mixed with guilt.

I told myself I would show her. Eventually. Just — not for a little while yet.

We took our trays and picked a place away from the heat of the south windows. It was an incredibly warm, brilliant afternoon, and the trees outside the building were like glowing clouds of lemon-yellow and scarlet.

When I looked up, I saw Smitty, sitting by himself across the room. The sight of him gave me a tremendous jolt.

"You're not listening," Hally said, following the direction of my stare. "Oh," she said, with some kind of meaning I didn't understand.

"I'm trying," I said, absently — but that wasn't true. The little paper in my pocket was burning. I put my hand over it and, totally on impulse, said, "I've got something that belongs to him. I'll be back in a minute."

As I made my way across that cafeteria, my chest started closing up on me. Suddenly, I was heart-riven and hard of breathing, and I honestly didn't understand why. I guess I should have listened. I guess I should have trusted my heart.

I came up behind Smitty's chair and glanced over at Hally, who was watching me curiously over the rim of her cup. Then I hunkered down beside the chair, sitting on my heels, and peered up at him. He, of course, took no notice of me at all. My hands went cold.

"Hi," I said, on no breath at all. "Listen," I said. "Caulder gave me your Machiavelli paper. This was stuck in it —"

His body went rigid.

"I thought you might want it back," I went on, lamely. And then stopped. Something was wrong, here. Incredibly wrong. "Anyway . . ." I murmured, and I pulled the poem out of my pocket and put it on the table in front of him.

He pulled in a breath and sat, frozen, for a fraction of a second. Then he shoved the chair back, nearly knocking me over. He swung around, pulled himself out of the chair, and — for just one breath of a moment — his eyes glanced across mine. And connected. Like an electric shock. Then he was gone.

I couldn't breathe. I couldn't do anything. His eyes were blue. Why didn't I already know that? And I couldn't shake the feeling I'd just seen Charlie inside of them.

Things had gotten very quiet on this side of the cafeteria.

I looked up and people all around the table were looking at me with profound surprise. But I didn't see any more than that; the truth had finally come to me. The truth about the poem. I glanced across the faces and found Hally's. It was like looking into a mirror, seeing the shock on her face. She canted her head sideways sharply. *You'd better follow him,* she was saying.

I had the presence of mind to snatch up the

poem, and I tucked it back into my pocket as I ran out of the cafeteria. I made it out of the door just in time to see him disappear around the corner, down the causeway toward the classroom building. I had to run to cover that ground before he had a chance to disappear completely.

I followed him down an empty corridor, around a corner, and down another corridor, trying to keep far enough away, so he wouldn't see me, but close enough not to lose him — all the time hoping I wouldn't run into any stray teacher who'd definitely want to know what I was doing in the halls without a pass. Then down the stairs, down one more hallway, and out the back.

This particular back door was taboo. The building was blind here, nothing beyond the door but grass and woods, and the principal didn't allow kids in that area for obvious reasons. The door was standing open.

Smitty had gone through that door and out.

I did not go through the door.

I leaned against the wall, breathing hard, and listened. At first, I couldn't hear anything but my own breathing and the blood pounding in my ears. I didn't want to move; I was scared I'd run right into him if I went out there.

I pushed away from the wall and drew close to the lintel, checking to make sure the hall was still clear. The classroom just to my left was empty. I felt like I'd fallen off the edge of the world.

And that's when I heard him. Somebody outside the door was in terrible trouble, sucking for air as though there wasn't any left in the world. I pressed my hand over my heart and leaned out just enough so I could see around the edge of the doorway.

Smitty was straight-arming the wall, not seven feet away from me, his face down between his arms, gasping and grabbing for air. *Asthma?* I wondered, frantically. *Is that what asthma sounds like?* I could feel the bricks under his hands prickling against my own palms. Smitty was smothering out there in the bright, clear autumn afternoon. I couldn't get my own breath, listening to him.

While I watched, his near arm gave way on him, and he folded up, his back to me, his shoulder against the wall, leaning heavily against the bricks.

I looked around wildly, thinking I should go get somebody. Get some help. But I couldn't leave. And what good would it do? Bringing somebody else into this would only make things worse.

Please, I prayed, deeper than I'd ever prayed for anything. *Please.*

I peeked around the corner again, my own legs gone to rubber.

He was squatting on his heels, his back to the wall and his head in his hands. His breathing had slowed down a little. After a minute, he put his head back against the wall and took one long, slow, weary breath.

I fell back against my own side of the wall.

So, he was all right.

Or, he would be, until he found me standing here, spying on him. I didn't dare look around that corner again. I just left. I walked back toward the lunchroom, feeling cold all over. What was I going to tell Hally? There was no question, she was going to ask — how could she not? The poem was obviously and absolutely not my business, and I didn't know how I was going to explain what had happened without having to explain that, too.

Driven out of first lunch. Now exiled from second.

What else could I do? I hid out in the library until I was nearly late for my next class, and I hid like a fugitive for the rest of the day.

"You're going to have to tell me," Caulder said. "I had to haul your purse all the way from chemistry to choir — and don't think I'm not going to hear about it for the rest of my life —"

"I *thought* she was being pretty weird," James said, looking at me appraisingly. They were *all* sitting around the dining room table, looking at me appraisingly.

"Hally wouldn't tell me anything," Caulder said, severely. "So I know it's got to be something cataclysmic." He sighed. That sigh was just one thing too many.

"Sorry I'm such a trial to you," I said, my voice gone all throaty.

"Come on," Caulder said, with a disgust that did nothing but make things worse. "Are you going to tell me what happened, or not?"

"Not," I said. Then I started to cry.

He groaned. "Ginny," he said, and he took my hands down from my face. "Come on." He dragged me out of the dining room, down the hall to the den, and stood there while I dropped myself on the good old couch and cried some more. He sat down beside me, perched on the edge of the cushions. "What did you do?" he asked, gently now, but still with an edge of weariness. Enough of an edge to light me a nice little flare of righteous indignation.

"Where did you get that paper?" I asked him.

He sat up straight. "Which paper?" I gave him this disbelieving look, and he gratified me by looking a little ashamed. He got up and went over to sit in my mother's chair.

"I got it out of Leviaton's trash," he said.

"*Caulder.*"

"Well, I saw Smitty chuck it, and I was curious." I just looked at him.

"So, okay," he said. "It was an immoral thing to do."

I was glaring at him.

"I'm *sorry*," he said.

"It was sneaky as sin," I said, sniffling.

"I know," he said.

"He didn't expect you to do that," I said, wiping at my cheeks with the butt of my palm. "It was a violation of his privacy. It was a violation of his *trust.*"

"I know," Caulder said again, beginning to sound gratifyingly miserable. "So," he said, warily. "What happened?"

I had to tell him. I started slowly, and I told him a lot of it, leaving out things I couldn't have said if I'd known how — about Smitty's eyes and my own final conclusions. I didn't do a very good job with any of it; I'm not that good with words, so the story came out sort of dry and plain, and left me feeling unfinished.

Caulder had closed his eyes.

"I was afraid he was going to die, Caulder," I said. "You should have heard it."

He shook his head.

"You know how you said we ought to push him?" I said, softly. "Caulder, listen to me. He's a real person. I'm really scared. Whatever this is, I don't think we have a right to be messing with it."

He was studying me in silence. "May I see the poem?" he asked after a minute. I didn't want him to ask that.

"I know," he said, not knowing. "But, please?"

In the end, I got it out for him. He handled it very gently, read it through — first quickly, then again slowly, and again, working out the words. He looked up at me. "Where do you think he got this?"

"What do you think?" I said, sidestepping him.

He frowned. "I don't recognize any of it."

"Maybe he copied it. Maybe he found it. Maybe somebody gave it to him. Maybe his *mother* wrote it."

"Maybe not," Caulder said, wryly. He looked over the poem once more, his face changing, and then he looked up at me, wonderingly. "You think he wrote this himself, don't you?"

I didn't answer.

"Which would explain why he came so unglued when he found out you had it. Except not. Why? Why would he write something like this and then throw it away? If he does stuff like this, why haven't I ever seen any? Why hasn't his mother ever said anything about it? Seems like, the way she is, she'd have had this published in *The New Yorker* by now." He looked at me again. "If she'd known about it. Which she evidently doesn't."

He sighed, looking down at the poem. Then he

107

handed it back to me, reluctantly, I thought. "We're in over our heads," he said, for once agreeing with me. "So . . . maybe we ought to go talk to that shrink."

Now he'd gone way beyond agreeing. "It's none of her business," I said.

"What if she just wants to help him?"

"Maybe he doesn't want help."

"Maybe he *needs* it," Caulder said. "Geez, Ginny."

I folded my arms and stared at the rug.

"What's wrong?" he asked. "I mean, what's really wrong? He's sick, Gin. There's something wrong with him. He writes stuff like that, but he never talks to anybody. He needs help."

"Whose help?" I flashed. "And once it starts, is anybody going to remember to ask him how he feels about any of it? He doesn't *want* to talk to her. Don't you think he's been very clear about that? If he wanted her to know anything, he could write it down like this and *send* it to her. But he doesn't, does he?" I just couldn't bear it. "Look at him. What if she hurts him?"

"Why would anybody hurt him?" Caulder asked me, softly.

"We did. We have. I have. Me." I was crying again, but it was different this time, strange. Tears were just welling up in my eyes and spilling over and there wasn't anything I could do about it.

"Just keep in mind," I told him, "we shouldn't have known about this in the first place. I mean, do you think he expected somebody to go around resurrecting his trash?"

"I said I was sorry," Caulder pointed out.

"What I'm saying is — I don't even know what I'm saying."

Caulder shrugged unhappily, maybe agreeing.

"He's not going to get over this one," I finished, miserably.

Caulder sighed. "He gets over it, Ginny," he reminded me.

I shook my head. "Not this time. If you'd been there, you'd know. Caulder, I thought he was going to die." I shrugged, and laughed this little laugh that had absolutely no humor in it. "So, I guess it's no big thing about the doctor, anyway, since he'll never let me get within miles of him after this."

Caulder cocked his head. "This is all my fault," he said.

"You're right about that."

He nodded slowly. "Okay," he said. He stood up. "See you in a few minutes." He started off down the hall.

"Wait a minute," I said, starting up off the couch.

He stopped and turned to me. "What are you going to do?"

He shrugged. "I'm gonna talk to him."

"Oh, uh-huh."

"Fine," he said. "I'll be back."

"Caulder," I said, following him halfway down the hall. "And just what do you think you're going to say to him?"

He shrugged again and grinned at me, pulling on his coat. "What does it matter?" he said. "You know he's not even going to let me in the house."

As it turned out, we were both wrong.

CHAPTER NINE

Caulder would never be quite sure what it was he'd said right. But then, if it hadn't been for Mr. Tibbs, Caulder might never have had a chance to say anything. Turns out, Mr. Tibbs has no problem with letting kids run around his house unescorted, as long as the wife is out on business, so Caulder had surprised Smitty in his upstairs inner sanctum, and said whatever it was that he said. "Now, we'll just have to see what happens," Caulder told me, afterward. And then promptly forgot about the whole thing in a fit of lovesick nerves, enduring the hours until Hally's party.

I was thinking about Hally's party, too. About how I wouldn't know anybody there. About how I'd been spending all my time and energy on Caulder's world without building anything of my own. Not that I was sorry about being with Caulder. It's just, I missed having friends — our parties back home, tame as they might have seemed to some people, had been pure adventure: You never knew who you'd meet there, or what might happen. Maybe something wonderful.

"They only give you a little time to live," Paul used to say to me. *"I don't know about you, but if I'm going to be going somewhere, I want to be driving the bus."* I sat

out on my lawn that afternoon, looking up at my trees, thinking the whole thing over. The trees had finally gone completely yellow. Their trunks were still damp and dark with the last night's chilly rain, black against those clear yellow leaves. I looked up at them, feeling like I was seeing reality, distorted through ultraviolet eyes. *It all depends on the spectrum,* I thought. *On what you're used to — what you expect.* I hadn't expected anything good for a long time. And I had to admit, these trees were a kind of beauty I'd never have been able to imagine on my own.

"They're almost done," James said. He jumped the fence into Caulder's yard, a cheese sandwich in one hand, sweater over his arm.

"Who?" I asked him, squinting into the late afternoon light.

"The folks. Dad told me, this morning. Have fun tonight. We're not going to be late." James gave me a wave and disappeared up Caulder's front steps.

Almost done.

Now, there was an idea — parents and children in the same house again. Normal life.

Suddenly, I was tired of sitting there. I was tired of just sitting around, waiting for my life to happen to me. I had a party to go to. I didn't even know who I was anymore — I hadn't even seriously looked in a mirror for weeks.

So, I went inside and I looked, and I spent the rest of the afternoon trying to bring the image back up to standard. When Caulder finally showed at my door, he had on a new sweater, deep green, with a plaid shirt under it, and his hair was all perfect; he was radiating joy and nerves. But in the midst of all that, he looked at me and dropped his jaw. "Geez, Ginny," he said. "I never saw you wear *that* before."

"It's just a dress, Caulder," I told him. I cinched up the belt another notch and did a little turn to make the skirt ripple. "See? Nothing exciting."

"But you look like you did it on purpose. I mean, you look — I mean, your hair —"

I smiled at him. "Same to you, Caulder," I said. And then I turned him around, gave him a push, and followed him out to the car.

He held the door for me, still staring. "I want you to watch who you talk to tonight," he instructed me. "I mean, you never know who's going to show up there —" Now, I was grinning. This was doing me a lot of good. "What about Smitty?" I asked him, though tonight, for the first time in weeks, it was not my consuming concern.

"Don't know," he said, belting himself in. "I told him we'd stop. I guess we'll have to see."

Smitty wasn't waiting on the walk. "Oh, well," Caulder said, and tapped the horn a couple of times, just for the heck of it. The door opened, and Smitty came out. Caulder looked back at me, giving me a silent *well-what-do-you-know?* I got out of the car, pulled the front seat over for Smitty the way I always did, and he slipped into the back. But he was not as he always had been — his face was the same beautiful blank, but he had lost balance, somehow. The air was crackling with it all the way up into the hills; I could feel the kinetics in the hair at the back of my neck. Caulder didn't seem to notice a thing.

It was a longish drive up to Hally's. The house

was perched up on the shoulder of the foothills, surrounded by trees, tucked back away from the street. As you started down the long driveway, you could see how huge the place actually was. For the second time that night, Caulder's mouth was hanging open, and he was looking distinctly uncomfortable. The party was downstairs in the back, where the bottom floor opened onto a patio and a bunch of little decks. The door stood open, light pouring out of it onto the patio, and the windows glowed like Christmas. We could feel the music when we got out of the car.

"Oh, my grace," Caulder said, soberly, taking a look around. "It didn't look this big from the front. 'Course, it was dark the other night." There was a deep yard behind the house. Toward the back, the lawn rolled gently down the hill; the tiny lights of the town blazed up beyond and just below through a lacing of trees, cold and twinkling. Hally'd told me her father kept horses in the meadow down below the yard.

Caulder took a deep breath and blew it all out in a single stream. "Well," he sighed, tugging at my hair, "come on."

We crossed the deck, Smitty trailing along behind us, and passed through the open door into the warmth of Hally's house. I still wasn't ready for the size of that room. We stood uncertainly in the doorway, staring at a massive fireplace that took up one entire wall, the kind of place you'd have hung huge iron pots, back in the days when they roasted an entire ox for lunch. All the furniture had been pushed back against the walls, and the middle of the room stood empty, ready for dancing. There were chairs and love seats tucked judiciously into shadowy corners, and a whole wall of obviously catered refreshments.

"Hello-hello-*hello!!!*" Hally said, sweeping us up. She pulled us into the room and introduced us to her brother, who was hovering over the stereo system. Then she dumped us at the refreshment table with an admonition to make ourselves at home and eat a lot.

Caulder drooped. I wanted to explain that he should be patient and let Hally get things going, but the music was too loud for talking. So I just grinned at him and started filling my plate. The table was like a gastronomic Disneyland — silver trays draped with doilies and mounded with little sandwiches, tarts, bits of fruit, and fancy things that bore only a faint resemblance to food as we know it — tiny pastel rolls, stacked triangles, and layered shapes, stabbed through with surreal, plastic toothpicks.

There must have been a hundred people invited to that party. They came in twos and threes and they kept coming — the boys gravitating toward the table or the stereo, the girls very pointedly and cheerfully not noticing them. All of a sudden, for the first time in months, I felt completely comfortable in my skin. When I caught a wink from across the room — a kid I recognized from my chemistry class — I laughed out loud.

From that moment on, I left Caulder and Smitty on their own; tonight was not my night for baby-sitting. Hally finally rescued Caulder, who instantly perked right up. Smitty was sitting in a chair across the room from me, tipped back against the chair rail, drinking punch out of a little crystal cup. He was almost faceless in the half-light.

A couple of girls from our English class came over and talked to me. Every so often, I'd catch somebody from the stereo clutch giving me the eye. The music was great; I was getting a tremendous rush out of it. And there was absolutely nothing weird going on, nothing to fear in the shadows, no limits on what magic might happen. Caulder was still casting the occasional worried look my way; whenever I caught him at it, I gave him a little wave. He shouldn't have worried; that night, there wasn't a boy in that room I couldn't have handled.

Except one. It happened when I drifted across to the refreshment table, weaving between the dancers, and shifted my focus from the party to the food. I was just ferreting out a few of the little pink and green rolls, when somebody close behind me said "hi," quietly in my ear. I turned around — it was a reflex — and nearly dropped the plate. Pete Zabriski was standing there. Smiling uncertainly at me.

"What are *you* doing here?" I asked, like an idiot. My eyes must have been huge, and I was hoping my mouth hadn't dropped open. Suddenly, I was not at all inclined to eat.

"I tagged along with my brother," he said.

"You did?"

"I wanted a chance to talk to you," he said.

"You *did?*"

"Yeah," he said, laughing. "Why are you so amazed?" He reached around and took the plate out of my hands. "Come on," he said, heading for the chairs. I followed, happened to catch Hally's eye, and looked daggers at her. She sent back a look of pure disclaimer.

"Sit down?" Pete offered, standing by a private and plush little love seat. I sat, suddenly all hands, hips, and teeth. I was beginning to feel a little seasick, actually. I could tell what was coming now. He was going to start to say something, and then I'd interrupt him, and then I'd be talking, saying absolutely stupid things, and not be able to stop, and then I'd start giggling like an idiot — your textbook social nightmare.

"I think maybe you've been avoiding me," he said. He really did have wonderful eyes. They were all crinkled up just now, because he was teasing me, because he *liked* me, I suddenly realized. "You didn't have to do that."

"I didn't."

"Huh-uh. Unless it was because you don't like me or something."

"Ummmm —" shrug. Stupid, shocked little laugh. Freeze up. Oh, wonderful. "How long have you played French horn?" Desperate.

He laughed. He had such a nice laugh.

"I'm not as stupid as I sound," I said, blushing but trying to get my balance back. "I just didn't expect to see you here." And with a rush of honesty — "I never would have expected you to talk to me."

"Why not?" he asked.

"Because I humiliated you," I said.

He laughed again, and then he kind of blushed. "Actually," he said, "I thought it was kind of flattering." Oh, he was too cute.

116

"So, I'm serious about the music," I said. "Is it a passion with you? Or more like a discipline? When I see somebody stick with an instrument, I always wonder about that. With my brother, it's definitely passion —" Suddenly, we were talking. Suddenly, I was sitting next to a living, breathing person — who kept *looking* at me. And people were looking at us, and I liked the way it felt. I *loved* the way it felt. But just about then, something started tugging at me, something in the back of my mind that kept casting fretful shadows.

Pete asked me to dance. This, I had been waiting for; I love dancing — my whole family loves dancing. Pete, it turned out, didn't dance very well, which was a little disappointing.

In the fade of that song, in the flickering shadows beside the hearth, Pete took my hand. It was then that my nagging shadow suddenly developed a face.

I glanced around. Smitty wasn't in the chair anymore. I scanned the rest of the room.

"What is it?" Pete asked me.

"I just —" I squinted, peering into the corners. "I can't see Smitty anywhere."

"Oh," he said. "That's right. Somebody told me you and Caulder came in with The Alien."

"His name is Smitty Tibbs," I said.

"Yeah," Pete said. "No offense. It's just — he's kind of a spooky guy."

"Well, you're right about that," I said. I'd pulled my hand out of Pete's, not even realizing it. "Excuse me a second," I said. And then, trying to explain to us both, "I'm kind of responsible for him."

"Should I help?" he asked.

"No. It's okay. I'll be back in a second, okay?" I had presence enough to smile at Pete before I left him. He didn't look exactly pleased — which, to my surprise, I found a little annoying.

I looked everywhere. I even checked the bathroom — well, I mean I went down the hall, and I saw the bathroom door was open, so I figured he wasn't in there. My nerves were beginning to kick in.

Finally, I left the house and went out onto the deck. I hadn't realized how loud the music and the energy in the room had been until the door closed behind me and cut them off. A chill breeze had come up, rattling through the leaves over my head. I stood against the rail, shivering, and then I closed my eyes, resting myself in the sudden solitude. Then I slipped silently down onto the driveway. I walked up to the street, a dark fear growing inside me. What if we'd lost him again? What if, this time, something terrible happened to him? I couldn't see him anywhere on the street, so I turned around and followed the drive back into the dark yard, wondering if I ought to go in and get Caulder. It had been a mistake, bringing him. I couldn't figure out why we'd done it.

I was freezing. I couldn't imagine anybody voluntarily coming out here for anything, not even for romantic privacy.

Then I saw him. He was sitting out at the end of the yard, a solitary and dark shape against the distant, frosty lights of the town. I stopped, feeling the heavy beat of my nerves. And suddenly, I was washed with a great, warming anger. I walked across the lawn to where he sat, my movement silent below the million tiny thunders of colliding leaves. I could still hear laughter from inside the house, still feel the bass and the beat of the music, muffled and distant — something like the darkness in the backseat of the car. Smitty out here. Almost close enough to the living to be part of it.

He was sitting on the grass at the far, rolling edge of the yard, and he was staring out into the night. He didn't move at all when I sat down beside him.

I wondered how long he'd been out here like this — no coat, no gloves — and I wanted to shake him. If this boy could write about Machiavelli, he could sure as heck exercise a little common sense. Obviously he wasn't helpless, he wasn't stupid; he was acting like an idiot, when it was clear he wasn't one. And I was beginning to feel like I had been playing right into whatever the game was. No more. I had had enough.

"There's a party in there," I said to him, working to keep my voice quiet. "There are people, talking to each other, touching each other — laughing. Did you see me dancing? Or did you leave before that happened? I love that, Smitty. I love the dancing, and the people talking. I love it. I belong there. But you couldn't let me stay, could you? You had to come out here and sit in the wind like an *idiot*, like there isn't a brain in your head, and *why*? What are you doing out here? Running away? Feeling sorry for yourself?"

He sighed and started to get up. My anger surged, and I turned and grabbed a fistful of the front of his sweater, pulling him off balance.

"Grown-up people don't just get up and *leave*

119

every time things get a little tight," I snapped. "I'm sick of this, Tibbs. I don't know what your problem really is, but don't you think it's about time you grew up? Don't you think it's about time you stopped using people? It wouldn't hurt you to take a little bit of responsibility for your own life. You can't run away forever — you're not *insane*. Some day, you're going to have to *respond* to somebody."

His face had gone hard, his breathing quick and shallow. He blinked, and he turned his face away from me. I put my hand under his chin and pulled his face back to me.

"*Look* at me," I said fiercely.

And he did.

He looked me straight in the face, his eyes full of shock or fear or anger — *something*. They were alive inside. *He* was alive inside.

I saw it, and I did something that took me totally by surprise.

I kissed him on the mouth. And I kissed him hard. It had been a long time for me, and a lot of passions I couldn't have named went into what I did — a kiss pressed hard against lips that might have been dead. It was too weird.

And then it got weirder.

Because the life inside of him suddenly suffused us both. Suddenly, I was no longer alone in the kiss, not the only one speaking strange passions. I could feel his hands move across my back, and then his arms went around me, for a moment, as though it were around my whole soul.

But I couldn't maintain it. When I felt the need inside of him, deep and dark and powerful — as if he were pulling out of me more than I had, trying to fill up the awful void he had been — I wanted to back away. But I couldn't do it; and that scared me the way nothing in my life had scared me. I could not break off.

He was the one who stopped it. He put me away from him, eyes closed. Both of us were breathing hard. There was anguish in his face.

"I'm sorry," I whispered.

He opened his eyes and looked at me. I couldn't move. I couldn't say anything more.

"Ginny," he said. He said it. He *spoke*. "Go."

No more than a hoarse whisper, but the words were distinct.

"Go now."

But I still couldn't move.

And then, as from his very soul, *"Please."*

I went.

CHAPTER TEN

"What *happened?*" Caulder asked.

We were back in the hallway by the bathroom, and I couldn't talk to them. They'd seen me come in, Hally and Caulder, and followed me back there, hovering around, wanting to help — but I couldn't talk. To Hally, that wasn't important; she just put her arms around me. But Caulder wouldn't leave me alone.

"Go on into the bathroom and blow your nose," Hally told me. "You can have some privacy in there at least. I'll come and check on you in a minute."

If Hally'd aimed a hint at Caulder when she mentioned privacy, he missed it completely. He followed me right into the bathroom and shut the door, and then he sat down on the sink counter and folded his arms. I turned around with a wad of paper under my nose and my eyes streaming.

"Ginny," he said, "you're scaring me. Did Zabriski try something? Because if he did, I'll kill him."

"Oh, Caulder," I moaned, and I closed the top of the toilet and sat down on it. He started to say something, but I held up one hand, blowing my nose with the other. And then I took a slow, deep breath.

"I don't know how I can tell you this," I said, and I meant it. How are you supposed to explain something to somebody else, when you don't even have the words you'd need to explain it to yourself? My heart was banging around inside me so hard, I was nearly dizzy — and now I was supposed to be able to untangle all these dark, weird feelings . . .

I made a try at it, just talking about looking for Smitty, and then finding him, and then what had happened, all the time begging him with my eyes not to make it any worse than it was.

When I finished, he just sat there. I screwed up my courage and looked him in the face. He was staring at me. "How do you *do* these things?" he said. "I can't believe you *do* these things."

I sighed and sagged against the wall.

"You got him to *talk* to you," he breathed. "You know what I'd give to have him talk to me?"

I laughed, in spite of myself. "Not the right stuff, evidently," I said.

But his face, studying mine, was very serious. "I can't believe you actually kissed him. How could you do that?"

"I wasn't just messing around, if that's what you're afraid of," I said, and I was angry. "I was sitting there with Zabriski, not five minutes before. If I'd wanted kissing, I could've gotten it there. And if I'd wanted to torture Smitty there are a thousand easier ways."

It got very quiet.

"Don't you think this is a little weird?" He asked.

"No," I said. But I was lying. What I had done

tonight had separated me from everything normal, even Caulder, and I was very scared. I blew my nose again.

"So, where is he?"

And then I realized — gone, probably. Gone again.

"I left him outside," I said, feeling like I was caught in a bad dream.

Caulder left the bathroom on the run. I caught up with him out in the backyard. Of course, Smitty wasn't there.

Caulder swore. I'd never heard him do that before. "Well, we've got to find him," he said. "Come on." I waited in the cold while Caulder got our coats. He had Smitty's, too. "Pneumonia," he said to me, holding it up. "Let's go."

For the next two solid hours, we searched — every road, every field, Hally's neighborhood, the hillside.

"I don't know how these things keep happening," Caulder finally said between his teeth. "Ginny, you make him crazy."

"*I* make him crazy? *You're* the one who wanted him pushed. *You're* the one who thought he'd been having it too easy. This should make you very happy. You were right — we pushed him up against the wall, and he finally had to react." I was crying again. "Isn't that what you wanted?"

He hit the steering wheel with the palm of his hand.

After a minute, he said, "Yes. That's what I wanted." He turned down another street. "I'm sorry." He went on softly. "Maybe I didn't believe anything would ever happen." And then, a moment and another turn later, "And I didn't know how it was with you." He glanced at me, but I couldn't look him in the face.

"You think I knew?" I asked him. "You think I know now?"

"Ginny," he sighed, "you've got to stop crying. We've got to find him, and you're not going to be able to see a thing if you don't stop."

We rode around for another half hour before we decided to go home. It had been so long, now, he'd probably gotten home hours ago. And we didn't know what else to do.

The second we pulled up in front of Caulder's house, his mother came out on the porch, one hand up, shading her eyes against the front light.

"Oh-oh," Caulder said. And if it was possible, my stomach did one more ugly twist. Caulder stopped the engine and got out.

"Park it," his mother said. "And then you'd better get in here."

He got back into the car, slowly, and we shared an awful look.

"I guess he got home," Caulder said, starting the car back up.

"Let's *hope* he did," I said. I could hear blood on the road in Mrs. Pretiger's voice.

Caulder pulled the car up into the driveway. "You'd better go home," he said to me as we got out. "I'll call you when she gets finished with me."

"I should come," I said.

"Go home," he told me, "and wash your face."

When the phone finally rang, it nearly scared me to death. I'd been curled up in a corner of the

125

couch, chilling and freezing in spite of the quilt I'd wrapped around myself. Miserable. My parents weren't home yet; for once, I was glad. The boys were already in bed and the house was still as death.

"How you doing?" Caulder's voice sounded tired.

"Not great," I said. "What happened?"

"Smitty got home way before we did," Caulder said. "He nearly froze to death on the way. And by the time he got home, he was really crazy. His mom called over here, thinking I could tell her what was wrong, but, of course, we weren't home, yet. She told my mom that Smitty was up in his room, throwing things around. Then, while they were talking, he came down and started pacing around from room to room, waiting for her to get off the phone. Mrs. Tibbs said his hair was standing all up, like he'd been pulling on it or something. She was crying when she called.

"She called about three more times, looking for us. My mom called Hally's, trying to find us, but we weren't at the party, either."

I moaned. "So, is he okay, now?"

"Actually, he's gone."

"Gone?"

"The last time his mother called, she said they were taking him over to the university clinic."

I didn't say anything. I just kept shivering.

"He wanted them to, Gin," Caulder said. "He wrote down the name of the psychologist himself, and he handed his mother the phone. My mom is really mad at me. She was just worried for so long, tonight."

I felt so cold.

"I guess I got what I wanted," he said before he hung up. "I hope he lives through it."

It was not an easy night for me.

I heard my parents come in, heard them messing around in the kitchen. They were louder than usual, laughing a lot. It was comforting, knowing they were there, and I wished I could just get up and go in and talk to them about it all.

But it was too late for that. I wouldn't even know how to start. What was I going to say — "While you guys were off doing whatever it was you were doing, I got involved with this dysfunctional mentally ill kid and, last night, I made a sexual move on him that finally drove him over the edge and now he's in the mental hospital?"

I turned over on my side, feeling sick to my stomach. *Why did I kiss him? Why did I have to kiss him?* At the very least, it had been a bad decision. If it had ever actually *been* a decision. And, no question, there were going to be terrible consequences. Everybody was going to have to know what finally set him off. They were going to have to know about me and what I'd done.

This was a nightmare.

And it was all my fault.

CHAPTER ELEVEN

Everybody stared at me when I came down for breakfast. I didn't have to look to know my face was swollen and my eyes were still red.

"You all right?" my father asked me, looking concerned.

"Fine," I said.

"Are you sure?" he asked me. It's actually kind of a coded question. It means *I know you're not fine, but I'm willing to respect your privacy — just remember, no matter what, you can talk to me.* But I wasn't comforted much, because I wasn't at all sure I deserved that kind of courtesy.

"You'll be glad to know," my mother announced, flicking a look at me, and exchanging one with my dad, "we're finally finished. Christianson Graphic Design is now up and running."

"So, now we can buy food?" Charlie asked, grinning.

"Eat all the pancakes you want," Mother said. "And after you finish, we've got boxes to unpack, and pictures to hang, and screens to scrape, and storm windows to get up —"

James stared at mother, his fork halfway to his mouth.

"Welcome home," Dad said, grinning.

Caulder showed up about halfway through breakfast. We made a place for him, but he wasn't any more hungry than I was. He also looked almost as bad as I did. There were some more quick looks exchanged between my parents.

"Did something happen?" I asked.

"Dr. Woodhouse called," he said, glancing around the table at the rest of my family.

"They don't know," I said.

"Know what?" James asked, then he did a little jump, like somebody'd kicked him under the table.

"She wants to talk to us," Caulder went on. "She wanted to know if we could come by later this afternoon."

I pushed my plate away.

"I told her we'd come," he said.

"And where is this you're going?" my father asked, carefully disinterested.

"The university clinic," I said, looking at Caulder. Now, my hands were shaking.

"The Mental Health Studies clinic," Caulder amended.

"Oh?" my mother said, her voice perfectly casual.

"It's about Smitty Tibbs," Caulder said. "He finally went off the deep end last night." He flicked his eyes across mine. That was all he was going to say.

My mother had dropped her hands into her lap. Her face had cleared a bit. "That's too bad," she said, quietly. "Are you two all right?"

I nodded. Then I shrugged.

"We just have to go and talk to his psychologist," I said. I kept my eyes on my pancakes.

"Well, maybe you can help him," Dad said, and

I could feel him watching me. You could almost hear what my parents were thinking — *Something's very wrong here. Something we should know about. We were wrong to leave them on their own for so long.*

"Maybe we can help," I said, but my voice didn't sound right. Maybe if my parents had been around more, I might have been talking to them all along, and things might have been different. Maybe they could've helped me to see things more clearly. Maybe not. Maybe this was just something I had to work through on my own. Except it wasn't like I was in this all alone.

Charlie was watching my face. He smiled me forgiveness — and he didn't even know what was wrong.

The clinic was a big, impressive, modern building — lots of dark glass and red brick. The trees out front softened the institutional face of it a little, but I was still sick, going up the walk to the door. I took Caulder's hand. I know mine was cold and damp. I couldn't feel his at all.

We stopped at the front desk, and I let Caulder talk to the woman behind it. She directed us to Dr. Woodhouse's office. I wondered if she'd been told to watch for us. I wondered where Smitty was, if he was okay. My hands felt like they were going to sleep.

I should have been home with my family, doing family things, and finally settling in. I'd waited a long time for that. But here I was, walking down a corridor in a place that was as cold to me as the moon, feeling trapped.

"We don't have to do this," I said to Caulder.

"For Smitty," he said.

"For Smitty," I echoed, feeling the trap close.

The psychologist's office door had no window. It was just a plain wooden door with a nameplate hung on it. Caulder knocked. I didn't hear an answer, but he opened the door and waited, politely, for me to go first. In my heart, I cursed his manners.

It was a warm-looking office; my father would have called it country-appointed: chair-railing, dark wallpaper with a tiny light print, plants, old prints, unhospital-like comfortable chairs.

The doctor was seated behind a large oak desk. The Tibbses were sitting in two of the chairs, off to the side. When I saw them there, I wanted to back out the door and run. Another two chairs were pulled up more or less in front of the desk so that they faced both Dr. Woodhouse and the Tibbses. These chairs were for us. Not a comfortable situation.

The doctor looked tired. Mrs. Tibbs's face was as swollen as mine, and it was hard-looking. Mr. Tibbs was angry; it was in his eyes, and all over his body. They hadn't looked at us when we came in, and they still weren't looking at me. My hands were hard on the arms of my chair, and I kept my eyes fixed on the desk.

"Thank you for coming," the doctor said. Her voice was low and calm. I was thinking, *She's a psychologist — she can probably see right through me.*

"How's Smitty?" Caulder asked. I glanced up at the doctor. She had a nice face.

"I think he'll probably be just fine," she said. It

was a careful answer. I wanted to ask her where Smitty was, if we could see him — but with the Tibbses there, I couldn't speak.

"If you'll forgive me," she said, "I'm going to get down to business." She looked at me, and I dropped my eyes. "I need to understand," she said, "how you two view your relationships with Smitty."

"We're friends," Caulder said.

Mrs. Tibbs made this wry little noise. I knew what she meant by it. She didn't believe anybody could really be Smitty's friend.

"Okay," Dr. Woodhouse said. Then she turned to me. "What about you, Ginny?" she asked. Her voice hadn't nailed me to the wall — but the question itself had.

"This is all my fault," I said. There wasn't any point in prolonging things. But I couldn't say any more.

The doctor was studying my face. I couldn't stand it. "Is there something wrong with me?" The question burst out of me. "Does the way I feel about him mean that I'm — is it wrong?"

Mrs. Tibbs drew in her breath.

But I was looking at the doctor. I needed an answer. Because I hadn't understood my feelings for a long time now, not from the beginning — not about last night, or if I felt the same way now, or about what was going to happen now.

"Do you care about him, Ginny?" the doctor asked.

"Yes," I said. "I mean, I care about what happens to him. Is that the same thing?" There was a box of Kleenex on her desk. She gave it a little push in my direction.

"I think it's good to care about people, don't you, Ginny?" she asked. She smiled at me. "I guess, what I need to know is," she said, "if you two are willing to help him."

"Absolutely," Caulder said, answering so certainly for both of us.

But I was still sitting there, shocked; she'd moved right past me. I'd been so certain I was the crux of the whole thing, and she'd passed me right by.

"Now, understand," the doctor said. "If you get involved with this, you're going to have to consider it an absolute commitment. We have to keep Smitty's emotional environment as stable as we can for the next little while. I can't have you jumping in and out on me."

"No problem," Caulder said. "What do we need to do?"

I looked at him, blankly. That word she'd said — commitment. It had kind of disconnected my brain.

The doctor looked at the Tibbses. Mr. Tibbs glanced at his wife and then nodded at the doctor. Mrs. Tibbs got up and left the room.

"Well, first you need to understand some things." Dr. Woodhouse folded her hands on the desktop. "We had a long talk with Smitty last night. I know that sounds pretty incredible, and no, it wasn't easy for any of us."

She rubbed the tips of her fingers over her eyes. "He told us a lot of things, including his own version of what happened at the swimming pool — I understand you're acquainted with the story."

Caulder nodded, staring at her.

"We can't tell at this point how close Smitty's

perceptions come to reality. So, let me caution you that what I'm going to tell you is *his* side of the last fifteen years. I don't yet know how — accurate any of this actually is." She looked at us, waiting for a sign we understood.

"Okay," Caulder said, slowly. We were moving a little bit too fast for him, too.

"Okay," the doctor said, and she placed her two hands flat on the top of her desk. "I don't know how much you know about abuse."

I didn't want to hear this.

More than anything in the world, I *didn't* want to have to hear this.

But she went right ahead and told us. She told us all about how Russell drowned two-year-old Smitty in the pool when nobody was looking. About how Smitty never told anybody because Russell had hung over his bed in the hospital and told him he'd kill him again if Smitty ever said another word to anybody. Dying once had evidently been enough. And Russell had said all that — *done* all that — right under his parents' noses. He didn't stop there, either. He punished Smitty every day of his life; little miseries, tiny tortures, making himself Smitty's only envoy to the rest of the world. He'd even made Smitty believe he'd put a bomb in Smitty's brain, a bomb that would go off if Smitty ever said a word or touched anybody when Russell wasn't around. All this mixed with *such* brotherly love — just enough patting to keep a little boy completely enslaved.

"Why didn't he tell somebody?" I asked, very quietly, but feeling like I had screamed it.

"Because he believed," the doctor said.

She spread her hands slightly, a kind of shrug. "Little children have a very tenuous relationship with the world," she went on, sadly. "They're just learning how things work, what the rules are. Russell started teaching Smitty the rules when Smitty was very young. Why would Smitty have questioned them?"

"But what about his *parents*?" Caulder spat, and then took a quick, embarrassed look at Mr. Tibbs.

Mrs. Tibbs had come back into the room and was standing by the door.

Mr. Tibbs spoke, his voice quiet, as if he were holding his feelings in very hard. "Russell told Smitty he was an orphan. He said we bought him at a garage sale, along with an old set of tires. He said he didn't want him touching his mother or me. And so, he never could."

"Russell was a good baby-sitter," Mrs. Tibbs said, her voice stiff. "We saw no sign of any of this. It's not as if we didn't pay attention to our children. I'm a good mother. I've always worked hard to balance my work and my domestic roles. I could have been working full-time — I could have had a good job. But I chose to stay home with my children . . ."

"Okay, Maggy. Okay — everybody knows you're a good mother," Mr. Tibbs said, not looking around at her.

She stopped. She stared at the back of his head and color came up into her cheeks. Then she lifted her chin and went on in this quiet, controlled voice. "We had good doctors; they were certain Smitty had brain damage. We tried to work with him, but the harder we pressed, the further away he went.

He has not been an easy child. It's strange to me that this story should be coming out now, after all these years. If there was any truth to it at all, we would have noticed something. And it would have come out long before this."

Mr. Tibbs turned around heavily in his chair and looked at his wife. "Just don't forget. You've got *two* sons," he said. She looked like he'd slapped her. And they held a glare between them like they were trading fire.

Caulder and I traded a quick glance. I really wanted to go home.

"Well, okay," the doctor said, quickly. "We don't know exactly where the truth lies. We're hoping to get to that point, eventually. What we have to concentrate on now is helping Smitty to integrate what is inside of him with what's outside."

"Well," Smitty's father said, shifting in the chair. "We should have brought that boy in here years ago and gotten this out into the open — "

"The only reason we're here, now," Dr. Woodhouse said, getting things straight, "and the only reason why we're having any success with him at all is because Smitty decided, himself, to come to me. Because *he* decided it was time. If he hadn't been willing, there might have been serious damage done. I can't tell you how deep these things go."

She unfolded her hands and folded them again the other way. She looked at us. "His relationship with you two — especially with you, Ginny — has been eroding his distance from the world. So, yes, in a way, it is your 'fault' that he's here. Because of whatever it is that exists between you, he finally had the courage, or the desire, to come in here.

The decision he made last night, coming here, was more significant than you understand. He took a tremendous risk. The moment he began to talk to us, Russell's bomb went off; we very nearly lost him."

"What are you saying? He nearly died? Last night?" The color had drained out of Caulder's face. I knew well enough what she was talking about. I'd nearly seen it happen out behind the school.

"I don't understand this," Caulder said, shaking his head. "You can't die from *talking*. Are we talking about voodoo, here? Are you saying Russell has some kind of parakinetic powers or something?"

"Not Russell," Dr. Woodhouse said. "Smitty did it, himself. The body is very obedient. What the mind believes, the body will often make reality. People who are sick, if they believe they're going to die, often do — on the other hand, if they believe they'll live, that can change conditions in their bodies dramatically. We're working with a group of patients now on reconstructive imaging as one of the approaches to healing their cancers.

"Being alive is a very complex thing. My science is not an exact one. But I'll tell you, I'm convinced that each human being more or less builds his own reality. You are what you believe you are. We make images in our minds of what will be — based on what we believe or want, what we're afraid of — "

"So, what you're saying is Smitty nearly killed himself so Russell wouldn't be wrong?" Caulder asked.

"Yes, more or less. What Russell had taught him got built right into the hardware, so to speak, and when he triggered it, his body did what he believed it would or should do. Does that make sense?"

Caulder nodded slowly, frowning, and sat back.

"Okay," the doctor said. "That's the background. Your job has nothing to do with Russell. Your job will be to teach Smitty that he doesn't have to die just because he wants to be alive. Okay?"

Caulder nodded. But I couldn't imagine what she thought we were going to be able to do. And I was not at all sure I wanted anything more to do with this.

"Where is he?" Caulder asked, quietly.

"I'll take you down there in a minute. Give me a minute, and then we'll talk some specifics."

She shooed us out of the office with orders to wait for her down at the end of the hall, and then she closed herself in again with the Tibbses.

"Come on," Caulder said, tugging at the back of my jacket.

I stumbled around and followed him. "So, this doesn't this scare you?" I asked, numbly skipping a few steps to catch up.

"What I want to do to Russell scares me, if that's what you mean."

That's not what I meant.

I'd almost killed Smitty once — maybe twice — by doing the wrong thing. It could happen again — it probably *would* happen again. And that scared me. And I absolutely didn't want to have anything to do with the Tibbses' ugly secrets. I just wanted to live my life and do my math and write notes to Hally.

But it was more than that. More basic. More selfish. I'd had some of these feelings before —

you go out with a guy because you think he's nice, and maybe, after a little while, you let him kiss you — or maybe you kiss him — and then, all of a sudden, everything changes. All of a sudden, he thinks he owns you, he thinks he's got these *rights* to your life and your thoughts and everything you do. The chances are, *you* didn't mean that much by it in the first place, or maybe it turned out, after you got to know him, you didn't really even *like* him all that much. Maybe he's even repulsive to you, now — but it's too late. Because he thinks what he thinks. Because you let him think it, at least for that one moment. And now feelings are going to get hurt, and it could be very ugly. And when you get down to the truth, you're the one who made the mess.

But this. This was so much worse. We weren't just talking about feelings here — we were talking life and death. We were talking a guy in a hospital who could die just by *thinking* the wrong way. And it wasn't just between Smitty and me; people I didn't even *know* knew every little detail. They all knew what I'd done when I'd kissed him, and they *all* felt like now he should have rights to my life. Like I'd sold my soul, and I didn't even know who it was I'd sold it to. Because I really didn't know anything about Smitty, about what he was inside. And I was not at all sure I was going to like what I found there.

"What if I hate him? What if it turns out he's somebody disgusting?" I said, not even meaning to speak it out loud.

"Come on," Caulder said, giving me a look.

"I don't like this," I said. "I don't like this." I don't

think I was even aware that Caulder was standing there. I think I was beginning to panic.

"Don't you think it's a little late for that, after last night?" Caulder asked, and there was a flash in his voice of what sounded like anger. And then I knew he was there; I knew it because I heard those words and something exploded in my brain. I had never hated anybody in my life the way I hated Caulder at that moment.

I stopped walking. He went on a ways before he realized I wasn't with him. Then he turned and looked at me.

"I don't have to come back here," I hissed, my eyes burning holes in his face. I meant what I said. Nobody could make me do this. For once in my life, I didn't care if every human being in the world hated and despised me.

Caulder started to say something, then evidently thought better of it. He shifted his weight and waited.

"This is not . . ." I said, but I was running out of coherent thought. "I don't like any of this," I said between my teeth.

"It's not a game anymore," he agreed, as if _I_ had been the game player in the first place. We stood there, glaring at each other.

"Shut up, Caulder," I told him. "You have no right to say a word."

He folded his arms and looked away. He took a long breath and lifted his chin a little, and when he looked at me again his face had changed.

"Would you really leave him in this place all alone?"

The doctor's door opened. We watched her

coming down the hall toward us. "Okay, guys," she said, once she got close enough. "Let me tell you what I'd like you to do." She kept on walking, and Caulder fell in behind her, looking back over his shoulder at me. I drifted along behind them, not committed either way.

"I'd like to see you here as many afternoons as you can afford. The more time you spend with him, the quicker things are going to settle out. Okay? All I want you to do is just be there with him. Do the best you can to treat him and each other the way you would in a normal, everyday situation. Except you have to keep in mind that emotion — especially his own — is a language he just doesn't speak yet. Don't expect him to pick up anything subtle. And be nice. And patient. But don't patronize."

She stopped outside of a closed door. "Keep in mind he's under sedation, and he's tired. We're going to keep this visit very short. Do not expect *anything* from him today. And no interesting incidents, please." She was grinning when she said that — but she was looking at me.

Smitty's room was a lot like the doctor's office, meant to look like an old-fashioned bedroom. I think that was supposed to be comforting, but against that wallpaper, the big hospital bed with its sterile white sheets and chrome railings was disturbing.

Smitty was in the bed. The sight of him was deeply shocking to me. It was like he'd starved overnight, wasted away. His eyes were dark smudges on a still, pale face. There were wires running from his body to the monitors over against the wall. The room was full of soft beeps and electronic hums.

He seemed very fragile. I wondered how I could have felt threatened by this.

He opened his eyes as we came in, and seemed to watch us. But I don't think he was seeing much; an IV bottle hung right above him. Even so, under that empty look, Caulder slowly came to a stop, his eyes silver around the edges.

"Hi," Caulder said, softly.

Smitty closed his eyes and breathed a deep sigh. Caulder glanced at the doctor. She nodded and led us out of the room. "It'll get better," she said, stopping in the hall. "He seems to be a tough-minded kid. If we can just get that toughness working for him instead of against him — " she lifted a hand and then dropped it. She smiled at us. "Real friendship can be very healing."

"How long is he going to be here?" Caulder asked.

She shrugged. "Long as it takes. So. See you Monday. Check in with me when you get here. Any questions? Okay." She smiled again, and then she turned around and went off down the hall. We went down the hall the other way, neither of us saying anything. Caulder held the door for me as we left the building.

"So," he said, carefully. "Is she going to see both of us on Monday?"

I shrugged. "I gotta get my math done, some way."

He laughed, like he was letting off a breath he'd held too long. "You had me worried for a minute, back in the hall. I'm glad you're sane, now."

"Thank you," I said, but I was thinking he shouldn't go jumping to conclusions. I was going to be seeing that silent face in my dreams for a long, long time.

CHAPTER TWELVE

I told my family the story.

Not because they asked — but because they didn't. I told them because I needed to tell them. I couldn't tell them exactly everything, because of the fact that I didn't understand everything, and I left out a lot of the end, including the kiss. If I was sure that what I'd done was immoral, I'd have told them about it and felt better. But what I'd done was only strange, so I had no such relief.

They were very supportive. And, of course, they expected me to act in a mature, responsible, and philanthropic manner; the weight of it made me tired. But it was only what I had started expecting of myself, the moment I'd seen the waif in the bed.

The first thing the doctor did when we got to the clinic on Monday afternoon was to show us the equipment. She took us into an empty room and showed us a monitor like the one they had on Smitty. "Not that I think you'll need to mess with it," she said. "But you never know." She showed us how to read the meters, how to tell when we should be going for help.

If she expected the demonstration to bolster up my confidence, it didn't work.

"Don't push him," she said to us, finally. "Don't

talk about the situation. Don't bring up his family. Talk about school. You talk. Don't expect him to. He's having a hard time matching up the vocabulary in his mind with the feeling of the moment. It'll come; he's incredibly bright. But for now — I suspect he feels very much at a disadvantage. Maybe even humiliated in front of you all. Think of how you'd feel. And remember, he's still somewhat sedated. Just be kind. Be normal."

Caulder rolled his eyes at me as we followed her down the corridor. Be normal. Of course.

"Okay," she said, pushing open Smitty's door for us. "Good luck."

For once, Caulder didn't stand back and let me go first. He was too passionate about this. I could see Smitty over Caulder's shoulder as I followed him into the room. "He's asleep," Caulder whispered to me. Heaven knows the kid looked like he needed it. Smitty's face was still absolutely shocking. He was like something out of a refugee camp, hollow-eyed and drawn.

He wasn't asleep. His eyes had opened when Caulder whispered. He watched us as we came softly into the room, his face unreadable as ever. Caulder saw those eyes and froze, staring. They were looking at each other for the first time.

Caulder cleared his throat. "I'm sorry all this stuff happened to you," he said, his voice gone rough. "I hope you don't mind that we're here."

Smitty didn't answer. His eyes flicked across mine and then away. He closed them again and he sighed, a long, slow breath. "Come in," he said, finally, and for a moment, I was afraid Caulder was going to faint. You could hear the medication thick in Smitty's voice. He sounded like he was trying to talk through a dream.

"I'll get some chairs," Caulder said. I took a step toward the bed, and then another. Smitty's eyes were still closed.

All I did, I swear, was touch his hand. The way he looked was so pitiful, and I didn't stop to think. I just reached out and touched him.

Alarms went off. Immediately, his body went rigid, and suddenly he was pulling his breath in hard down his throat. The monitors went absolutely haywire and Caulder flew out of that room on the wings of panic. I jerked my hand away and stood there like an idiot, staring down at Smitty.

The whole thing didn't take longer than a second — one of those kind that feels like years. Then, head pressed back into the pillow and chest heaving, he was trying to bring himself back. His hands were clenched in the sheets. You could feel the tremendous effort he was making for control.

And when he finally opened his eyes — what did he see? Me. Me with my mouth open. Me wishing I could drop right through the floor and die. He kept his eyes on me for only a second, breathing like he'd run a long, long way, then he closed them again. He let go of the sheets.

Caulder and the doctor came in like the cavalry to the rescue.

It was the first thing I had done. The very first.

Smitty sighed. The doctor stood in the doorway for a moment, reading the monitors. She nodded at Caulder and left. She hadn't even looked my way. My cheeks were flaming.

"Geez, Ginny," Caulder said, scowling at me.

And then he looked at Smitty. "Are you okay?" he asked. I'd never heard Caulder's voice like that, so gentle. I was beginning to think Smitty hadn't heard him when Smitty finally gave a little nod.

"Good," Caulder said. His eyes turned silver again and he started messing with his notebook.

I stood there watching Caulder — I had to look at something — and then I swallowed, and made myself look down at Smitty. He was not looking at me.

"I'm sorry," I said. I felt so stupid.

He didn't answer me at all, but some color came up in his cheeks.

Caulder was sitting way out on the edge of his chair with his hands kind of clasped together between his knees. I sat down in the other chair. I didn't know what to do with myself.

"I've been wanting to talk to you for so long," Caulder said. But then he said, "Forget it." He picked up his world history book and started leafing through it. "Forget it. We're supposed to be doing our homework."

Smitty just lay there, breathing, staring at the ceiling, one hand lying over his heart.

Caulder spent the rest of the time reading to us out of the world history text while I drew pictures in my notebook. I didn't belong here. I was only making things worse. But when I thought about not coming back, it made my heart sore.

We'd been there about forty-five minutes when Caulder took a quick look at his watch and got up. While he put the chairs back, I put on my coat. Caulder picked up my books and gave them to me, and then we stood beside the bed.

147

Smitty looked up at us vacantly. "Not necessary," he said, his voice slurred and ragged.

"What isn't?" Caulder asked.

There was a long pause. "Coming here," he said.

"You mean us?" Caulder asked, sounding surprised. "You don't want us to come anymore?"

Smitty said nothing.

"I hope you don't mean that," Caulder said, putting one hand on the bed. "Are you saying you don't want us?"

Smitty closed his eyes. "No," he said finally. And then, "Come."

"All right," Caulder said. "That's what we were hoping."

Smitty didn't look at us again. "Okay," Caulder said. "See you tomorrow."

Silence.

Caulder led the way out the door. The doctor met us in the lobby. "How'd it go?" she asked. She was looking at me.

"Maybe I shouldn't come back," I said. I was right on the edge of embarrassing myself; I had to keep blinking. It wasn't like the doctor couldn't have told how upset I was.

"Don't you want to?" the doctor asked.

"That's not it," I said. "I don't think I'm going to be any good at this. I'm afraid" — I shifted my books around and fixed my eyes on the woman sitting behind the desk across the room — "I'm going to end up slowing things down."

The doctor reached out and patted my arm. "I think you ought to keep coming," she said. "I think he wants you to. Trust me. It'll get easier. Okay?

It will. I'm almost sure. Come tomorrow. See how you feel then."

Caulder kept talking at me, all the way home, trying to cheer me up. But he didn't understand. I couldn't say much back to him.

And then, of course, the family wanted to know how things had gone. I told them that Caulder thought we'd had a grand success — he and Smitty had held their first conversation. Smitty had said three things. It was all a miracle to Caulder.

"You didn't connect with him yourself," Charlie guessed later that night, when we ran into each other in the hall outside the bathroom.

I stopped and leaned against the wall, hugging my robe around me because I was so cold. I'd been cold like that all evening. "Worse than that," I told him. "I made a total fool of myself, Charlie. I hate being a jerk, I just *hate* it." And then I told him what happened. It was almost the hardest thing I'd ever done, trying to talk about it. "After that," I said, keeping my voice as level as I could, "he wouldn't look at me. He wouldn't even *look* at me."

Charlie sucked his toothbrush thoughtfully.

After a minute, he pulled the toothbrush out and pointed it at me. "Maybe," he said, "he was embarrassed. Maybe that's why he wouldn't look at you. Think about it. Everybody's treating him like he's a psycho case. And then he spazzes out in front of you. How's he going to feel? Especially if he likes you. I think he's probably totally humiliated. I would be."

And so would I. I'd never thought of it that way.

"If he has any normal feelings at all, he must feel

totally weird about himself," Charlie said. He started into the bathroom. "And always remember the male ego," he said, grinning. He gave me a little wave and closed the bathroom door.

I did a lot of thinking that night. I tried to climb inside of Smitty's head and see things through his eyes. It was very difficult. *You don't know this person at all,* I told myself. *Not at all. And you're so full of yourself, how will you ever learn anything?* I figured out, finally, I was going to have to forget everything I ever knew, forget everything I had ever assumed or expected. This was a new thing, something I had to learn. Because I wanted to.

So, I did go back the next day, holding on as hard as I could to Charlie's perspective. I tried to forget myself. I took a completely passive attitude; I watched. Over the next couple of days, I began to pick up on Smitty's new language. A sigh, a change in his breathing — how stiffly he held himself, whether he was looking at us or not, the amount of sheet he had wadded up in his hand, the tiniest tightening around his eyes or his mouth, these things began to take on the significance of a shout.

But things weren't coming along fast enough for Caulder. I think what he'd expected was some kind of sudden awakening on Smitty's part. "How are you feeling?" Caulder would ask. Or, "What do you feel like doing today?" Or, "How's the food?" He was expecting answers and conversation and friendship. All he was getting was the occasional vague answer, and never to a direct question.

Smitty didn't look directly at us very often, but

you could tell he was aware of us. He was listening. Undoubtedly, he felt the waiting. The hovering. It really must have been painful for him, very embarrassing.

I tried to explain things to Caulder. "You're too impatient," I said. "We need to spend more time talking to each other, so he can hear us, instead of trying to involve him directly. You're pushing him too hard. Let me remind you, sonny — you can get real nasty if somebody pushes you when *you* don't feel like talking." But Caulder wanted to hear words out of Smitty in the worst way, and I knew what he was like when he had his mind set on something. There was no way I was going to talk him out of asking his questions.

So, one day, at the end of that first week, when we'd just come in and Caulder hadn't had a chance to take over, yet, I decided it was time for me to intercede. Praying that I wouldn't do anything wrong this time, I stood close to the head of the bed. "Smitty," I said, quietly, holding my books hard against my chest. "I don't want to bother you, but I wonder if you'd mind helping me with my math. I'm getting behind."

Smitty blinked at the ceiling.

"I wouldn't ask, but I really need the help." This was absolutely true. For four days now, all I'd had for help was Caulder. I was dangerously close to losing my grade.

When Smitty did a slow nod, I got a little adrenalin rush. Caulder pushed a chair into the backs of my legs just then, and I was glad to sit down. "Yes," Smitty said. They still had him on drugs, and his reactions were slow. He turned his head and he looked right at me for the first time since that night. It took my breath away.

"Yes, what?" Caulder asked, sitting down in his own chair.

"We're going to work on my math," I said, lightly. I bent over and put the rest of my books on the floor.

"Are you sure you're ready for that?" Caulder was asking him.

I sat up and glared at him. "Shut up, okay?" I said. Caulder was offended, of course. But he did shut his mouth. After that, it was interesting. We had to figure out how we were going to hold the book so everybody could see it, and where to put the notebook so Smitty could write — but so nobody would be touching anybody by accident.

Smitty had kind of pulled himself over on his side. That was the first time I'd seen him off his back. It was also the first time in days I'd seen him actually look at anything. A little color was coming back into his face.

I watched that face as he read over the problems, his cheek on his hand. I was still thinking it was a gentle face. He had a nice mouth — not soft, but sensitive. His lips were pursed slightly now, as he tried to focus on the work. His eyes were still very dark, and his hair was wild.

He picked up the pencil and began to write.

"Talk," I said, gently. "You can explain it to me in words, now."

Cheek still cradled on his hand, he looked over at me.

"You can do it if we go slow," I said. "I'll understand it better."

Without moving, he seemed to fade away inside of himself. But after a moment, he came back. "All right," he said.

Caulder was sitting there next to me, listening to us with fierce intensity.

It took a long time for Smitty to get through that first problem. It was a whole new way of thinking for him. It really was like he had to translate from one language to another before he could speak. It made him hesitate in funny places, looking for a word, or the turn of a phrase. He was very shy about it. But he did well. And the second problem was easier.

When we finally left that day, Smitty spoke a quiet good-bye.

I felt good. I felt like I'd done it the way Charlie would have. I had connected, and it hadn't hurt me, or Smitty, or anybody.

I hardly even noticed how quiet Caulder was, all the way home.

CHAPTER THIRTEEN

After we'd been hanging around the hospital for about a week and a half, I finally decided to tell Charlie everything. From the beginning. Not leaving out a thing. Not sparing myself any humiliation. I needed to do it; it was time I got somebody to help me.

"What I don't understand," he said to me, when I'd finally gotten through it all, "is why you're so ashamed about what you did. Did you kiss him because you were trying to shock him, do you think? Or were you just frustrated? Or was it just the flaming of a sudden passion?" He grinned at me.

"It was not flaming passion," I said. At least, I didn't think it was.

"Emotions are so complicated, aren't they?" he mused. "They're never pure and simple. I guess you just have to be as honest as you can. I think you have to follow your heart, Ginny. Look — you've got an unusual thing going here — you've got a chance to build a real relationship with somebody. There are people who never get that kind of chance in an entire lifetime. Listen very hard, and follow your heart. Your heart is good. It's your brain that gets you into trouble. Anyway, I don't think you should be ashamed. I think you've been doing the best you can."

And when I thought about it, maybe he was right.

"We have some good news," Dr. Woodhouse told us, waving us into her office chairs the next Monday afternoon, "and some of the other kind. The good news is we've been able to cut way back on the medication. He's handling himself better, and he's becoming more and more articulate. We're making this progress because he wants it. And he's working for it. He's a lot more comfortable string-ing words together, now. And that's going to make it a lot easier on everybody.

"The bad news is this: We can get him to talk about what he remembers, and we can get him to talk about his parents, or about his brother, or about school. But we can't get him to talk about himself. Or about you, evidently because his feel-ings about you are too deeply tied up with himself. Not that he actually *refuses* to talk about these things. He just doesn't respond when we get too close to home. He does refuse hypnosis. That was a flat refusal. First one he's made. Kind of refresh-ing, really.

"Knowing this shouldn't change what you all are doing. But I'd be interested in hearing your obser-vations about this stuff when you check out today. Okay?"

She never should have said anything.

Please understand, Caulder is a wonderful person — wonderful, faithful, true, and all that kind of stuff. But as I've said before, he's very stubborn about getting what he wants. And he started in on Smitty the second we walked in the door.

"How you doin'?" Caulder called, swinging through the door like he was on some kind of holy mission. He dropped his books on a chair and started to tug it over toward the bed.

"Hiya," I called softly, watching Caulder with foreboding.

Smitty turned his face to us and one tiny corner of his mouth lifted. It was wonderful. It was amazing. If Caulder had been in his right mind, that would have been enough for him. But I don't think he even saw it.

Caulder dropped into his chair and leaned toward the bed. "I want to know how you feel today." He said it with fixed intensity, like a bird dog on point. I was left to bring my own chair over, so I didn't see the answer on Smitty's face. Smitty hadn't said a word.

"Aren't you going to tell me?" Caulder asked. Subtle as a bulldog. "Okay," he said, when he still got no answer. "What's the problem?"

Smitty turned his face away from us and went totally blank.

"Tibbs, excuse me, but what're you doing?"

I slugged Caulder on the arm, but he was past noticing me. "Caulder — " I said, beginning to get angry. I saw the wonderful, fragile interchange we'd started the last session evaporating into the air.

Smitty's eyes were fixed on the ceiling.

"Listen — " I started.

"No," Caulder said to me, making a sharp movement with his hand. He leaned over close to the bed. "Knock it off," he said. He said it quietly but

156

his eyes were burning holes in Smitty's face. "Whatever this is, you gotta knock it off."

The needles in the monitor meters were beginning to dance nervously.

"What do you want?" Caulder asked him. "You want to live the rest of your life all by yourself? If there's something wrong, you can bet you're not in any shape to handle it by yourself right now. If there's something wrong — don't you think that's what we're here for? What do you think I've been waiting all these years for? I came here to listen to you. People talk about their feelings, Tibbs — that's what friends are for. You don't shut them out when things get hard. You shut down on us like this, and you're just telling us you don't want us here. That what you want to say? 'Cause if you want us out — we'll go."

Something quick came across Smitty's face.

"Go," he said.

But then he whispered, "Don't."

"Then you talk," Caulder said.

Shut up, I mouthed at him. He looked poison back at me. *"Back off,"* I hissed, and I meant it. Caulder threw himself back in his chair, his eyes still hot.

We sat there for a long time, glaring at each other. You couldn't have told what was going on in Smitty's head, except that the meters showed he was having a hard time.

And then he said something, finally, softly. The monitors peaked.

Caulder let his breath out slowly and looked at me. "What?" he said. And then he leaned in toward Smitty. "Say it again?"

157

A moment went by. "Not working," Smitty whispered. His breathing was ragged.

"Come on," Caulder said. "It's gonna work. You've just got to try. You're not trying. You try and you'll be fine."

I could see the tension in Smitty's jaw. "Fine?" he said softly. He closed his eyes.

Caulder blinked. I was still glaring at him.

"Caulder doesn't mean to bite," I said, not taking my eyes off Caulder's. "He's just stupid. And he apologizes. Don't you?" But I warned him with my eyes: *Don't open your mouth.* "He just wants you to get well, that's all."

Smitty let go of a breath. "To be normal," he said, after a moment. There was a strong tinge of bitterness in the words.

"Yes," Caulder said.

I added, "Whatever that means."

Caulder started to say something else, but I held up a hand and stared at him until he shut his mouth and threw himself back in his chair. It was so quiet in the room after that, Caulder began to fidget.

Smitty's eyes were still closed. "Not possible," he said.

"What?" Caulder snapped, flaming right back up again. "What's not possible? For you to be normal? Of course it's possible. Are you nuts?"

"*Caulder —* " I hissed.

He glared at me, but when he realized what he'd just said, his face went pale.

And Smitty said, softly, "Yes."

There was dead silence after that. For the moment, Caulder didn't dare open his mouth. Smitty still lay with his eyes closed, pulled back inside his pain. And I sat between them.

"Everybody's nuts," I said, finally, still glaring at Caulder, trying to heal the silence.

"My brother Paul always used to tell me that every person defines reality in his own way. And every person figures that anybody who doesn't agree with him has got to be irrational. Which is another word for nuts, right? So — " I shrugged, " — I guess it depends on whose reality you're using for rules. You just have to remember that, and then you can see that nothing should be taken absolutely seriously. Personally, I always like to use my own reality as a standard." I shot Caulder a mean look. "I know that Caulder really prefers his own."

"I'm sorry," Caulder said.

"You're not the only one with troubles Smitty," I went on, gently. "You're just more visible than most, right now."

"I'm really sorry," Caulder said.

"Will you shut up about it?" I told him.

"Her brother's right," Caulder said, doggedly. "We're all weird. We're all scared. My mom's scared to be happy. I'm scared — of just about everything. Of being a jerk — I can't imagine why. Look, I'm really sorry, okay? I'm just not very patient. I just want you to be well — okay? I just mean functional. So you can be happy. I don't mean normal. I don't even know what normal means."

Smitty heaved a slow sigh. Caulder went kind of sad and dreamy, staring absently down at his hands.

"Everybody makes mistakes," I said, talking because, somehow, the talk was helping — just the sound of calm voices, like a salve. "Sometimes life is really kind of stupid. But wonderful things can happen, too. That's why you want to be alive. Because wonderful things really do happen."

"Yeah," Caulder said and, suddenly, he was grinning to himself. "They certainly can."

"Like, what is it that you're thinking of?" I asked him, instantly suspicious.

He had turned into a perfect Cheshire cat. *"What?"* I asked, kicking at his ankle. Smitty had opened his eyes, probably because we'd temporarily forgotten all about him.

"Sometimes," Caulder purred, "you get to kiss beautiful, blond, nubile women." He batted his eyelashes at me.

It took me a minute to realize he wasn't just teasing me. When I finally got what he was saying, I nearly dumped the books out of my lap. "You finally kissed Hally. Why didn't you *tell* me?"

"Do I have to tell you everything?" he asked sweetly.

Smitty was looking at us, now. Looking at Caulder. "Was it good?" he asked, openly curious — just part of the conversation.

My mouth dropped open, and I stared at him. "I can't *believe* you asked him that."

Smitty looked back at me for a long moment. Then he blinked, and he said, "Some parts of me are normal."

"Oh, wonderful," I said, and I folded my arms and shoved myself back into the chair.

Smitty was still looking at me.

"It was great. It was very nice," Caulder said, and then he sighed, happily. "Her lips — "

"Would you just shut up?" I said to him.

Smitty's eyes were going thoughtfully back and forth between us. They settled on me. I noticed it after I'd given Caulder one more good, steel-edged glare. "You're mad?" Smitty asked, just to make certain.

"Not really," I said. "Just disgusted." Actually, all this talk about kissing had made me *very* uncomfortable.

Smitty made a soft, considering sound.

"What?" Caulder asked.

"Faces," Smitty said softly. He was looking at Caulder now. Then he moved his hand slowly so the edge of it crossed the plane of his vision. "They change — " He dropped his hand and lay back on his pillow. Caulder looked at me. I leaned over, picked up a textbook and handed it to him. The room was always so quiet when we stopped talking. The rustling Caulder made, riffling through the pages of the book, seemed very loud.

Caulder found his page and looked at me. He raised an open palm: *Should I read?*

"Paul," Smitty said softly, speaking to the ceiling, again. "What does he do to you?"

The question took me totally by surprise. And when I realized what he was asking, I could hardly breathe to answer. "Nothing," I said, trying to keep the shock out of my voice. "My brother has always been good to me. Paul — he's very gentle. He loves me."

He sighed. "I'm tired, now," he said. He sounded weary.

Caulder got up, awkwardly. "We've got to go anyway."

Smitty closed his eyes.

Caulder put the room back in order. I put on my jacket, and then I waited with my books in my arms.

"Okay?" Caulder said. He came over, balancing his own books. "See you tomorrow?" he asked.

Smitty opened his eyes, very drowsy-looking. "Tomorrow," he said, and closed his eyes again.

"Okay," Caulder said. He jerked his head toward the door. I went that way, looking back over my shoulder at the bed. Smitty was lying quietly.

"So what is this about you and Hally?" I asked, once we were out in the hall.

He gave me a face that was all innocence. He was messing with the collar on his parka, trying to pull it around straight.

"I would say that if something as serious as kissing has happened," I remarked, "the least you could do is let me in on it. Because you *know* — even if you don't tell me, Hally will."

"Does she tell you things about me?" he asked, like the thought had never before crossed his mind.

"Are you nuts?" I said, and the balance of power swung very nicely over my way.

"So, what does she say?" he asked, with a vain stab at nonchalance.

"It seems to me," I said, airily, "information like this ought to be worth something. You know? Some little — "

"Extortion," Caulder said.

"Ah," I said. "Right."

"Is it good, what she says?" he asked, looking a little worried.

I bumped him into the wall with my hip and ran for the car.

"What is your problem?" James said to me at dinner.

"What?" I asked, taking another bite of broccoli.

"You keep staring at everybody," he said. "And I wish you'd knock it off."

"I do not," I said.

"You kind of are," Charlie said.

"You kind of are," my dad agreed.

"It's like you think this is the last time you'll ever see us or something," James said. "It's making me uncomfortable."

"James — " Mother said. She doesn't like anything that smacks of portent.

"Well, she is."

So I made a face at him to make him feel better.

"How'd it go at the hospital?" Mother asked.

"Pretty well, actually," I said, stabbing at my potato.

"It'll go by turns," my dad said. "Sometimes it'll be good, sometimes not. You just kind of have to hold on through the bad parts, and keep on going."

Suddenly, I started to wonder about my dad, what kind of things he'd been through himself — how much there was about him I didn't know.

"She's doing it again," James said.

"*What?*" I glared at him.

"You should have seen the way you were looking at Dad," James said.

"Would you eat?" Mother said to James.

"How can I? How am I supposed to eat when she's staring at me?"

"I wasn't staring at you." And that was the truth — everything there was to see in James, you could pretty much take in with a glance.

"Ginny," Mom said, sounding tired. "Are you staring?"

"No," I said. "I'm just looking. And thinking."

"About what?" Charlie asked.

"I'm not sure," I said. "I think it's being with Smitty. All of a sudden, I can't take anything for granted anymore. I never realized how intricate it is, you know — interacting like this — it's like music, the way we sit at the table together — everything going back and forth, weaving in and out. Like a string quartet. And how you learn to understand each other. I've been doing this stuff all my life, without even thinking about it. I can't figure out how we learn it."

Charlie was looking at me thoughtfully. "If you start thinking too much about it," he said, "it stops working."

"You *were* staring," James pointed out.

"Did you know little kids can pick up foreign languages without even hardly trying?" Charlie went on. "Like, you move to Germany, and the parents are still trying to figure out the grammar while the kids are out there, already yelling at each other in fluent German." He shrugged. "The parents may never get it."

"Really," James said.

"PBS," Charlie said, citing his source, and went back to his meat loaf.

164

"So, maybe the key is," my dad ventured, looking at me, "just let this kid learn. Don't get all hung up on teaching. Show him, let him watch you guys, and don't make a big deal out of it. He'll get it."

"You're so wise," James said, grinning at Dad.

"Why, thank you, James," Dad said, graciously. "Perhaps some day, you will be, too."

"I doubt it," Charlie said, his mouth full of meat loaf.

"You'd better hope so," James said, huffy now. "*Somebody* in this family's going to have to be able to support Mother in her old age."

"Excuse me?" Mom said.

I loved it, the way she lifted her eyebrows. I wondered what she was like when she was my age.

"Look out, Ginny," James said. "You're staring again."

CHAPTER FOURTEEN

If I had to explain Smitty in one word, I think I would have to choose the word "quiet." This should not be read as tranquil; Smitty's "quiet" in those days, and for a long time after, was borne out of deep weariness and confusion. Some of it, the confusion, disappeared quickly enough, but his fatigue was soul-weariness — that has to be healed over time. And forever after, there would always be that quiet left in his face and his voice.

He had spent so long using his face as a blind that the delicate coordination of thought and movement, the impulses that bring a face to life and are second nature to everybody else, had to be carefully learned and practiced. His face was so sober at rest, a person could easily miss his sense of humor, which was dry and intelligent. Caulder made that mistake a hundred times, early on. Even so, anyone who was interested enough could have learned to read a full spectrum of meaning in Smitty's face. I was interested.

So when I say that Smitty smiled, what I mean is just the very barest tucking up of one corner of his mouth, hardly a movement at all. And when I say he spoke, or laughed, or even yelled — these were all shades of his ever-quiet voice. Everything he said, especially in those first weeks, was spoken softly. You could learn to hear the irony there, or frustration, or affection, or the occasional bitterness. But he always spoke so gently, you could miss all the meaning just by thinking you'd heard the words.

The best place to read his feelings was in his eyes. He had a very direct, unguarded, searching look. It could make you very uncomfortable, that look — as though he could read your whole soul.

When he was first learning to take charge of his own life, Smitty was still at the point where words didn't easily string themselves together between brain and mouth. He'd break his sentences in funny places, waiting for the language to catch up to the thought. If ever he spoke a good number of words together, you could bet it was something he'd been thinking over carefully before he ever opened his mouth.

It was a long time before Caulder understood any of this. He was too eager to hear, too impatient to watch and learn. In a way, it was the fact that Caulder was being such a pain that finally made Smitty take hold.

Caulder always started out our sessions the same way: "How *are* you?" he'd ask, always with the same look — like he was a cat fixed on a rat hole. He finally asked it one time too many. It was on Friday, the third week, that Caulder asked his question for the last time. Smitty blinked at the ceiling and answered, "How are *you*?" It was a simple evasion. But it was a beginning.

"I'm fine," Caulder said, dropping his books on a chair and looking Smitty over.

"I'm fine, too," I said. "Except for my math."

Caulder grinned at me. "Ginny's nearly hysterical. Zabriski finally called and asked her out."

"Pa-*lease*," I said, getting my own chair. Actually, I was feeling pretty good that day. I looked up and caught Caulder's signal — Smitty was watching us. I smiled at Smitty and moved my chair over close to the bed.

"This is what you wanted," he remarked, his eyes on me.

I grinned. I couldn't help it.

"It makes you happy," Smitty said. Maybe he was asking. It was suddenly kind of hard for me to sit still under that look.

"I don't know if it makes me *happy*," I told him. "But it surely does make me feel awful — *nice*."

"It changes your face," he said.

"Okay," Caulder announced. "Down to business." He folded his hands and fixed that stalking look on Smitty. "So, how are you, today?" he asked again, sounding very perfunctory, and giving me a definite warning-off as he said it.

Smitty heaved a tremendous sigh.

"Just give me an answer and we can get past this," Caulder offered.

"You don't have to give him a very serious answer," I added. "It's a customary question. Most people just say *fine*."

"Fine," Smitty said.

"That doesn't tell me anything," Caulder objected. "Besides, you don't look fine."

That was true. He'd looked tired at the beginning of this session. He seemed a world wearier now. He had turned his face to the ceiling again, away from Caulder's eyes. "I don't understand," he said after a moment, "why you *ask* me this."

"I want to know," Caulder told him.

Smitty folded his hands over his chest. "You think you have a right?"

"I'm your friend," Caulder said, catching fire a little. "And Ginny's your friend. That gives us the right."

"You can leave me out of this," I told him.

He gave me a sour look and went right on ahead. "We care about you. We worry about you. How else are we going to find out what's going on with you? That's why the doctor wants to know how you feel. How else is she going to help you get better?"

"How else," Smitty echoed.

"What I don't understand," Caulder went on, "is why you look so flipping tired all the time. You look like you haven't slept a night since you've been in here." Actually, Smitty had lost a lot of that waiflike delicacy we'd seen on him the first day. I mean, I was definitely still thinking of him in waif terms, and his eyes were still shadowed and sad, but now he had a little more weight and color in his face, and didn't look quite so ready to die.

"You said you have math?" Smitty asked, addressing the ceiling.

"Smitty — " Caulder said.

"I certainly do," I said, overriding him. I bent over to get my book.

"I just want to know how you *are*," Caulder insisted, ignoring me.

"Caulder," Smitty said, wearily, "you ask too much."

"What?" Caulder said. "What is the big *thing?"*

"Leave him *alone,"* I said. I dropped my trig book into Caulder's lap, hard. "One-fifty," I said. "Find the page." The monitors were telling us this was not a good situation, and you could hear the stress in Smitty's breathing.

"What is the *problem?"* Caulder demanded, shoving the book away. "Just *tell* me how you *are.*"

I turned on him and said, "I think he's trying to, if you'll just shut up and pay attention." And then Smitty began to talk.

"The problem is — " he said, speaking through his teeth, and breathing hard. He paused, taking a careful breath. " — being pulled into pieces. You want to know what I feel. They want to know what I feel. Everybody has a right. You ask me these questions — it costs me, Caulder. I can't answer you."

"It's a simple question," Caulder protested.

Smitty closed his eyes. He had a handful of sheet.

"All night," he said, his voice ragged, the words coming slowly, "the doctor and her simple questions. After that, my mother — pushing. And crying. Wanting something, I don't even know what. And then you. And then, after you, my father. In that chair. And never speaking a word. Waiting. He wants something. And then the doctor again." He reached for a breath. "And every afternoon, you." He had a tight hold on the sheet. "These questions — they cost me, Caulder. More than I hope you know."

There was a silence.

"Sorry," Caulder said.

"Normal people," Smitty said softly, "expect privacy."

"Sorry," Caulder said, again.

"I need help with my math," I said, firmly. I got no argument this time. I also got very little help. I finally read a problem out loud, and after a long time, Smitty tried to talk me through it. He never turned his face to me, but he finally let go of most of his sheet. Caulder didn't make another sound.

But he couldn't stand the chill-out for very long. "We should go," he said, as soon as I'd finished the problem. He stood up, gathered his materials, put his chair back against the wall, and began to pull on his parka.

I sat there, watching him.

Smitty stirred. "Stay," he said.

Caulder paused, his arm partway into the sleeve of the parka. He pulled the rest of it on slowly. "Okay," he said, and he sat down in his chair by the wall.

"Ginny," Smitty said. "Alone."

I saw the hurt in Caulder's face. "Sure," he said. "Okay. I'll wait out in the lobby." Caulder looked at me blankly and nodded once. Then he picked up his books and left the room.

It was very quiet after that.

"You hurt him," I said, finally.

Smitty winced.

"He really doesn't mean you any harm," I told him.

I looked past him, to the window. There was nothing to see out there except the light-gray sky and a few bright scarlet ivy leaves. Kind of a desolate view.

171

Smitty took a slow breath and began to speak, almost to himself. "I have read about every human condition. In reading the words, I felt that I understood them. I thought I understood them."

The monitors kept up their soft beeping, a faint sound in the corner of the quiet room. "It never occurred to me that it would be difficult to use them. This way. Speaking. I think in language — I write. I write well. It never occurred to me that speaking with another human being would be different than that." He moved one hand up along the sheet until it rested over his heart.

"I could have told you it wasn't that easy," I said.

"Too quick," he said. "And dangerous. You speak words that mean one thing in your mind, but once outside, they change." He closed his eyes.

I never knew what to do in the silences. I put my hands together and held my tongue, waiting. "I can't tell you," he said, finally, sounding tired as all the earth, "how much I regret that they ever pulled me back."

I opened my mouth, and then shut it before it finally struck me what he meant. "You mean, from being drowned? You mean — you don't mean — you're not serious."

He didn't answer. And that scared me. I'd had a friend back home who had talked like this for a while, this same quiet way — wishing she weren't alive. She finally ended up trying to do something about it.

"Smitty — " I said, standing up, moving closer to him.

"Michael," he said, softly, cutting me off.

I blinked at him. "What?" I asked.

"My name," he said. And then he looked at me.

"Your name is Michael?" I repeated, stupidly. "Don't you like to be called 'Smitty'?"

He studied me for a moment. "Smitty," he said, "is theirs." His hand was still resting over his heart. "My name is Michael." Our eyes met. I sat down.

"Not many people seem to know it," he added.

"You could've let somebody know," I pointed out.

His eyes were still on me.

"When I sign my name," he said, "I always use my name."

And with a jolt, I remembered the title page of that Machiavelli paper. Michael S. Tibbs, it had said. "Your middle name is Smith," I guessed.

"My mother's father," he said.

I sat back into the chair. "Do you want me to tell them?" I asked.

His eyes still holding mine, he shook his head slowly. It was private information.

"Not even Caulder?" I asked. Not even Caulder.

He turned away from me again.

"Smitty," I said, and then stopped. "Michael." He didn't look at me. He was being solitary, now. "You didn't mean that about wishing you were dead," I said. It just came out of me, out of my distress, out of my sense of his distance from us. "You know, you should never say stuff like that."

He smiled, still not looking at me. "And if the thought is there?"

"You just put it away from you," I said, standing up, feeling this terrible, helpless alarm. "You just don't think it. How could you not want to be here now?"

173

"Ah," he said. He went on with soft irony, "What hell could be better than this?"

"The point is," I said, leaning over so that I could see his face, "what's happened has happened, and okay, it's been horrible. And okay, it's been a nightmare. But it's over now. It's over."

He met my eyes, and there was bitter amusement in his. "Over?" he asked.

"Yes," I said, but I had a hard time meeting his look.

"Whatever may happen to me as time goes on," he said, "whatever I become, wherever I go — there will always have been this."

I let my breath go in exasperation. "But can't you just, like — rise *above* it? Go on with your life? Can't you just forget it and move past it?"

And then, into his eyes there came a kind of shock. "I don't think so," he said. He had been wise, all these years, never to have looked anyone in the face. His eyes would have given him away. And just now, I was seeing myself in them, and seeing how little I really knew about the world. My hands were shaking. I was way over my head here, and it made me feel very young, and very frightened.

"I don't want to hear this," I said. It was a reflex, something like throwing my hands up in front of my face.

He made a sound in his throat and turned his face away.

"You're scaring me," I pleaded with him.

"You don't want to hear me," he said.

And then I finally realized what I'd done. What Caulder had been begging for, and the doctor had been hunting — Smitty — Michael — he'd given it to me. And all I had done was turn it back on him.

I dropped into the chair. And I said to him, "That's not what I meant to say." I folded my hands in my lap. "I'm sorry. It's not what I meant."

The monitor went on with its gentle sound, regular and steady in the quiet that followed. The wind blew outside the windows and the red leaves danced and tapped against the glass.

"I have a tendency," I said softly, "to speak before I think." I was hugging my elbows in tight. "It's just, people — we do things wrong. All the time. We're awkward. And we hurt each other when we don't mean to. And we don't understand each other. Sometimes, we're so full of ourselves, we can't hear anybody else. That's me. I mean, that's what I'm like. And I shouldn't be."

He hadn't moved.

"Caulder asks you questions," I said, "because he knows you're hurting. And he hates that. He doesn't want you to be all penned up alone. He doesn't want you to be separate anymore. He wants you to let him be part of your pain, so he can make it less for you. He's just not very good at it."

Smitty. Michael. He sighed. And he turned his face away from the wall. Turned it to the ceiling again, but ever so slightly inclined toward me. "Caulder has been after me for a long time," he said, with some resignation. "He's very patient."

"He loves you," I told him. "He really does."

He made that soft remarking sound in his throat and fell silent. The leaves still danced against the window. When he spoke again, his voice was cold. "The doctor wants me. She can push very hard.

There are places I don't want her to go." His eyes were still dark. He ran a hand through his hair. "You," he said, more gently. "You needed me for a while." He smiled to himself. "I thought you did. That was hard for me." The smile faded. "You don't need me now. I'm the one who needs. This is harder."

I folded my hands into my lap, wanting to say something and not having any idea in the world what to say.

"I have to tell you." He sighed again. "It's very difficult for me," he went on, going carefully now, "to have you here every day." He closed his eyes against the words he was speaking. "I'm helpless." He looked to the window. "I am damaged. I'm weak. I am — " he moved a hand, slightly " — deeply ashamed, to have you see me this way. Ashamed is not a strong enough word. I would have had it be different. But — it's not." I thought he was going to look at me; he never quite made it. "You think of me the way my mother sees her charities."

"I don't," I said, softly.

A heartbeat went by in silence.

"It's difficult," he said.

"Are you saying you don't want me here?" I asked.

"Yes," he said.

My eyes stung. "Are you sure?" I asked, my throat closing up on me. "I know I'm not helping. I know I hurt you just now. But if you let me come, I won't do it again. You can tell me anything you want, and I won't tell you it's wrong. Please? Don't tell me not to come?"

He closed his eyes.

"If you send me away," I told him, going for

broke, "you'd be totally at Caulder's mercy."

There was no response for a moment. Then he smiled.

There was suddenly noise in the doorway, the clearing of a male throat. Smitty — Michael and I, we both jumped. It was Caulder, standing in the doorway with his parka on and his books tucked under his arm.

"I've got to go home," he said, apologetically.

Michael nodded. And then he opened his eyes and turned his face to Caulder. "Thank you," he said.

"Sure," Caulder said, looking a little confused. "See you tomorrow?"

"See you tomorrow," Michael said, looking resignedly at me.

Caulder didn't ask me anything as we walked down the hall on the way out. I thought that was brave of him. I wouldn't have known what to tell him, if he had.

"At least I got some of my math done," I said, by way of making conversation.

"By the way," Caulder said, sounding a little stiff — "I want to thank you."

"For what?"

"For never throwing it up to me what a jerk I am in there."

"How could I?" I asked him. "When I'm so busy being a jerk myself?"

That night, I told my family about Pete Zabriski. Of course, they greeted the news of this impending date with deep satisfaction. They liked nothing better than an opportunity to exercise their mob wit on the innocent and undeserving.

"You *are* gonna straighten your hair?" James asked me at dinner that night. He'd been chewing real slowly, kind of staring at me, leaning his cheek in one hand. It was not the kind of remark I felt bound to answer.

Charlie, thoughtful as always, warned me, "He might want to kiss you." My mother has never allowed us to say "shut up" at the dinner table. I smiled at Charlie and batted my eyes.

"Leave her alone, you guys," my dad said. "You'll get her nervous, and then she'll sweat, and then she'll *never* get married."

"I can't believe you said that." I glared at him. My own father.

He smiled at me sweetly. "I'm just concerned about your future, honey," he said.

"All *right*," my mother said. "Knock it off. How often does the girl go out that you should embarrass her like this." My mother, too.

"You are envious," I said, "because someone *hand-some* and good-*looking* — unusual traits around here thanks to our genetic drawbacks — wants the benefit of my company. A young man who is *cultured*, no less." I held up a hand, silencing James, who was — no doubt — about to ask if we were talking salmonella or streptococcus. "He plays the French horn."

Charlie raised his eyebrows. "He must — " he said, leaning forward over the table and looking very sober." — have *great* lips."

This was, of course, considered just incredibly humorous.

I considered turning the table over on all of them. I settled for pointed silence.

"I can see up your nostrils," James said.

Charming. And so appropriate at dinner.

"As it happens," I said primly, shaking out my napkin and placing it carefully onto my lap, "I haven't even told him, yet, that I would go." I looked up, daring anybody to say anything. Evidently, I was looking a little dangerous. I smiled. "It's so nice to have the family all together," I said. When I looked up, it seemed to me my mother had taken that comment just a little more to heart than I'd expected.

"Yes," Charlie agreed, with great relish — "it *is* wonderful."

CHAPTER FIFTEEN

As it happened, the date with Pete Zabriski turned out to be a complicated matter. We couldn't seem to settle on a day that was good for both of us. Mostly, *I* couldn't seem to settle. Couldn't seem to want to commit myself. Of course, I had a lot on my mind, and maybe that was the trouble. Anyway, we sort of decided on the night before Thanksgiving. It was almost three weeks away, but there was this, like, Homecoming thing that night, so at least we had an event to look forward to.

But like I say, I did have a lot on my mind. I'd finally decided to take a little independent affirmative action, so that Saturday, all on my own, I took Charlie to meet the person I now knew as Michael Tibbs.

The visit started out quietly enough. Charlie was very civilized and decorous while I was introducing them. Michael had never in this world expected me to be bringing casual visitors by, and he kept looking at me like he wondered what, under heaven, I was doing.

Then Charlie suddenly whipped something out of his pocket. "Cards," he announced. He fanned them against his palm a couple of times, grinning at Michael. "I bet you have a *terrific* poker face."

Michael raised his eyebrows. I'd never seen him do that before.

"You're on your own," I told them, neatly side-stepping any pitiful, pleading shots that might have come from the Tibbs eyes. And it worked out. They took to each other pretty much immediately. I spent the afternoon in a chair by the window, reading a book and feeling guilty about sneaking in here without Caulder, while Charlie taught Michael how to play canasta. And then rummy. And then five-card stud.

I think that afternoon did more for Michael than all of the sessions and visits and general torture he'd been through, put together. By the end of the day, Michael finally seemed to have lost all awareness of himself. He wanted to beat Charlie. And he thought Charlie was funny. They sat there insulting each other — after Charlie'd shown Michael how to do it. It was just two kids playing together. It was magic, and it was really beautiful.

I tried to explain the whole thing to Caulder that evening. I told him, we need to bring the light into that room, not fix on the darkness. And I don't know, I guess Friday's incident had finally humbled him up a little, because he listened to me without taking any offense.

Over the next couple of days, Michael really worked on forgetting who he was, where we were, who we were with, and what he had been through. And as the pressure came off, so did the medication. We all started breathing a little easier, Michael got more and more clear-eyed every day.

Like I said, he would probably always be a quiet kind of person. But as the days went on, he retreated less and less often into isolation. The shadows around his eyes disappeared. His sense of humor started popping up. He still wouldn't let me tell anybody but Charlie his name. I guess he had to keep something where he felt like it was safe.

And then came the day, about five weeks after Hally's party, when we found Michael sitting up. He was wearing sweats, his hair clean and rumpled up. He was reading *Reader's Digest*, which he closed as we came in, and dropped on the night table.

"Whatcha reading?" I asked him. I put my books down and pulled off my coat.

" 'Drama in Real Life,' " he said. When I looked at him, he was doing his lopsided smile.

"You look good," Caulder said. This was a nonthreatening version of the old question.

"I'm vertical," Michael said. "No drip," he added, holding up his left hand so that we could see there was no needle stuck in it.

"That's good," Caulder said, getting settled in his chair. He opened his world history text. "Chapter twelve," he announced, and started reading. I slipped down in the chair and let my eyes wander. There wasn't a lot to see in that room. For all the homespun wallpaper and prints on the walls, there was nothing in the room that could have told you it was Michael's — not a picture, not a keepsake of any kind, nothing on the dresser but that *Reader's Digest* and a new box of light-blue Kleenex. A souless place.

While I was looking around the room, Michael was looking at Caulder, studying him, one finger absently pressed against his lips. Caulder finally felt it. He forged ahead with the reading for a time, but in the end, he couldn't stand it anymore. He closed the book and put it down on his lap. "What?" he said.

Michael blinked once. Caulder waited. Michael sat back and folded his hands into his lap.

"What is it?" Caulder asked again.

"Ginny told me that you love me," Michael said, at last.

"That's right," Caulder agreed.

Michael looked down at his hands, and then up at Caulder again. "I don't understand," he said.

And then Caulder was mulling it over, trying to figure it out himself.

"Does it mean you want to control me?" Michael asked.

"No," Caulder said, looking shocked.

Michael lifted one eyebrow about a millimeter and nodded, thoughtfully.

"It means — " I started. But Michael held up one finger, cutting me off.

"Does it mean that you expect carte blanche with me?" Caulder shook his head. "Automatic forgiveness?" Michael was asking these things in that delicately shaded way he had. "Unlimited access to my mind and my body?"

Caulder was still shaking his head, his mouth hanging open. "None of those things. How did you come up with that stuff? That's not what I want. Geez. What brought all this on?"

Michael leaned over and picked up the *Reader's Digest* again. "My mother was in this morning," he said, riffling through the pages. "She said she loved me. You evidently mean a different thing." He sighed, closed the magazine, and dropped it on the bed.

Caulder's face tightened. "Yeah. I mean a different thing."

Michael gave him one slow, silent nod. "You did say 'That's not what I want.'" Michael was looking at him again. "What is it you do want?"

"Nothing," Caulder said.

Michael smiled.

"Caulder," I said. "You think about it for a minute. You want him to let you care about him. You want him to care about you. You want to share things. You want to be able to joke around with him, talk about stuff — real stuff. Stuff that means something. You want Mich — Smitty — " I glanced up apologetically. "You want to be friends. I think that's a lot to want from anybody."

"That's true," Caulder said, quietly, after a moment. "I do want all that."

"You have friends. You have *normal* friends. Why — ?" Michael parted his hands.

But Caulder had no answer.

"Friendship," Michael said, tasting the word. "Desire? Keeping? Holding? Ownership? Control?"

"*No*," Caulder said. He turned to me. "I don't own you, do I?" he demanded. "Just because we're friends?" But then he got confused. "We do kind of own each other. I mean — we're responsible for each other. We *are* committed."

"How contractual," I said.

"Shut up," Caulder said. "This isn't easy." He frowned down at his hands. "What do I want? I want Ginny to respect me. I want her to care about me even when I don't deserve it."

"Which happens all too often these days," I said.

"Please?" Caulder said to me. "It's not like I think I have a right to know every little thing Ginny has in her mind. Just because I love her, doesn't mean she has to *give* me herself — I don't *own* her."

Michael blinked and looked away. "I just wondered," he said. And then, "I don't understand the point of your interest in me."

"I don't either," Caulder said, finally. "And I'm getting the feeling it bothers you." Caulder looked at him closely. "Are you afraid of me?" he asked.

Michael's eyes met Caulder's. "I have been loved before," he said, softly. Caulder's eyes darkened. Michael moved his hand, maybe warding off further discussion.

"You don't have to be afraid of me or Ginny," Caulder said, firmly, almost with anger.

Michael smiled. "Ginny doesn't scare me," he said. "Ginny doesn't love me."

"You don't?" Caulder asked, turning to me.

I dropped my pencil.

"I don't know," I said. I bent over to pick up the pencil.

"Well, do you love *me*?" Caulder asked.

"Of course I do." That was easy enough.

"You are often angry with him," Michael observed.

"That doesn't mean I don't love him," I said.

"That's what I mean by commitment," Caulder said. "If you love somebody, you're loyal. You hang on to them through the bad parts, the hard parts. You stick by them."

185

"Do you love Pete Zabriski?" Michael asked me, those blue eyes suddenly plain, flat disks.

"No," I said. "I don't even know him."

"Then why do you want him?"

"I don't *want* him," I said. "I just think he's kind of cute."

"You want to be with him," Michael said.

"Maybe," I said.

"Never try to get a girl to tell you the truth about love," Caulder advised.

"Ah," Michael said. "And when you go out with him, this person who's kind of cute. If he wants your kiss. Would you give it to him?"

My cheeks flushed. Caulder was sitting back in his chair, watching — half-grinning at me. "It depends," I said. "Maybe."

"Depends," Michael repeated.

"On the circumstances." I opened my math book. End of discussion.

Caulder was still grinning.

"Could we change the subject, please?" I asked.

Michael moved restlessly. "My mother," he said, now very uncomfortable, "always wants to touch me. On my arm. On my face." His mouth tightened. "I don't want her to do it." He looked at Caulder.

Caulder said, slowly. "Touching isn't always the right thing. It's perfectly all right to object, if that's the way you feel."

"In my family," I heard myself saying, "we touch a lot. Hugging and stuff. I guess because we don't need a lot of space. Or something." The way Michael was looking at me, I got flustered. "Some people like it, some don't. I like it, myself. When

186

it's appropriate, I like it." I faltered to a stop.

Michael kept his eyes on me. "It's not the touching I have a problem with," he said. He picked up the magazine and started leafing through it again.

Caulder looked at me and shrugged. Then he picked up his book and went about finding his place in it. "Oh," he said, suddenly — using his finger as a bookmark. "I'm supposed to ask you — Hally wants to know if it's okay with you if she comes here with us one of these afternoons. Would that be okay with you?"

There was not much reaction to that.

"She said Marti Avery wants to come with her."

And then something very weird happened. One of Michael's eyebrows did its microscopic lift, and suddenly he and Caulder were looking at each other — exchanging this *meaningful* look — like they had never done before. Instant bond.

"Marti Avery," Michael repeated, "wants to come here?"

"Who's Marty Avery?" I asked them.

The communication between them deepened. And then that one corner of Michael's mouth came up, and Caulder had this grin on his face. Something palpably male was passing between them and I was shut out of it.

So okay. I might not know who this Avery person was, but I had a fairly good idea *what* she was. I felt a hard, hot flush of hurt.

"*You* tell her," Caulder directed.

Then both corners of Michael's mouth turned up. He broke the look with Caulder, stared down at his hands — actually grinning. His first grin. For Marti Avery. "She's — " he started, darting a look at Caulder. Then he closed his eyes. His voice had gone ever so slightly husky. " — the girl who sits on the other side of the room, one forward, in Hanson's class. The one with the long chestnut hair." He said the word *chestnut* as though he were tasting it.

Yes. Okay. I knew the one.

"The one who took the Tingen Medal in math last year," Caulder added.

"I don't really know her," I said. My own voice had gone somewhat cold.

"Yes," Michael said, the ghost of his grin lingering. "Well. Neither do I. Not personally." He looked over at Caulder once again and they reestablished contact. "You're lying," Michael said, and that sounded male, too.

Caulder put his hands up. "Truth," he said. He stood up. "Anybody want a Coke?"

"No," I said, and I went back to my math. My face was burning. I was angry.

"No caffeine," Michael said.

"You got it," Caulder said, dropped his book on the table and left.

Michael closed his eyes. His face was not quite back in neutral; he seemed to be working on it. He slid down off the bed and walked around to the other side of it. He leaned against the wall and looked out the window. There were only two leaves left that I could see, more brown, now, than scarlet. The light from the gray November sky was soft on his face.

I reached into my purse for my calculator. Actually, I had to empty most of my purse out before

I could find it. While I was putting the stuff back, I dropped my library card, which should have been in my wallet, and had to get down on my knees and reach under the bed for it. It was a horribly undignified-feeling position, me on my knees with my behind in the air — especially with visions of the shining, beautiful, nasty, and totally undeserving Marti Avery still shimmering in the electrified air of that room.

I got back up on my chair, picked up my wallet, and tried to work the card back into its little plastic pocket. And then I remembered the poem.

It was there, just under my hand. Smitty's poem. Michael's.

I drew it out. I dropped the wallet back into my purse. And then I sat there, holding the poem in my two hands while he stood by the window in silence.

"I have something of yours," I said, finally. I couldn't look at him. I didn't like him very much just then. I stood up and leaned over the bed, putting the poem down on the side closest to him. Then I sat down again and resolutely opened my math book. He picked up the poem and then leaned back against the wall to read it. When he'd finished, he dropped the little paper into the trash. Then he turned back to his window.

"How can you do that?" I asked him, shocked. Somehow, this hurt me almost worse than all that talk about little Ms. Avery.

He looked at me.

"That's a beautiful poem. It doesn't belong in the trash."

"That's where Caulder found it," he said, simply.

"But I don't see how you can just throw it away. Especially now."

Another Michael silence. "I don't need it, now," he said.

"I want it," I said.

He leaned over, fished it up out of the trash, and placed it on the bed for me. He gave me one of his deep, unreadable looks, and then turned back to the window.

"Come see out my window," he said, not bothering to look at me.

"No, thank you," I said, stiffly.

"You're angry," he said.

I shrugged, keeping my face cold. I kept trying to make sense of the problems I still held on my lap.

He made his little sound, his neutral, considering sound. "Then it's too bad you don't love me," he said. He might have been teasing. I looked up and met his eyes. But not for long. I sat back into my chair and studied his box of Kleenex.

"I might have been wrong about that," I said, finally. "It's just hard to tell."

I couldn't know what he was doing without looking at him, and I didn't want to look at him, and he didn't say anything for a long time.

"I have been trying to understand," he said, finally, speaking almost as if to himself, "what you did that night at Hally's. I've thought about it a long time, but I don't" — he paused — "understand what passed between us then. Tell me this. If we were not here, in this place, the way we are — if

190

it were another place and another time, and I wanted that kiss from you. Would you give it to me?"

"I don't know," I said. I was cold all over and my hands were getting shaky.

Then, after a moment, and very, very quietly, he said, "Would you give it to me now?"

"Are you sure," I asked coldly, "you wouldn't rather wait for Marti Avery?"

I heard him breathe out one long, quiet breath. I glanced up at him and found him still watching me, that one corner tucked up. "It is very complex, isn't it?" he said, sympathetically.

I didn't answer.

"Ginny," he suggested gently, "come look out my window."

My heart was pounding in my ears. "I can't," I pleaded. "I'm scared of you."

"Scared of what? Of me? Or of what I'm asking?"

"Yes."

"But you would kiss Pete Zabriski, depending on the circumstances."

"Pete Zabriski," I said, hugging myself, "isn't hooked up to a bunch of monitors."

A moment went by, and then he said, softly, "Neither am I."

I looked up, but I still couldn't meet his eyes. He hadn't moved in all this time. And then he put one hand out. "Come," he said. "And just look, if you like." It was as if he drew me to my feet. I was still hugging myself.

"I don't want to get tied up with you, Michael," I said. "I can't — I'm not responsible enough."

"So," he said. "You're thinking, if something goes wrong between us, something terrible will happen with me?"

"It wouldn't be the first time," I said.

"Ginny," he said, patiently. "Don't you understand that I'm far more likely to die of satisfaction than I am of disappointment? Look. Look at me." After a moment, I did. He had on that funny little smile. "I will make you a promise. If you break my heart. You'll never, never know it."

He surprised a laugh out of me.

He lowered his hand. So, I went and looked out of his window. The clouds were lowering, getting darker. I saw a girl in a red sweater walking across the almost empty campus.

Michael didn't move. He just waited. And when I looked up at him, he still waited. Then he touched my lips with one finger. It was the first time he had ever touched me.

"I live, still," he said. He smiled at me, a beautiful, rich smile that started in his eyes. It was a funny little kiss after that; neither of us knew quite how to go about it. After it was done, he put a quiet hand on my waist and fit me gently against his side. Then we made a different kind of kiss, not hungry and frightened like that night at Hally's. Very sweet. Calming.

"I can't *believe* it," Caulder spat from the doorway. We drew away from each other and turned to him, both of us a little off balance.

He was scowling down at the cans he was carrying.

"All they had was *diet*."

CHAPTER SIXTEEN

Charlie got to see Michael one more time before it all hit the fan, and that was a good thing for Michael Tibbs. Charlie tends to act on your immune system a little bit the way a good shot of B vitamins will. Just the thing if you're headed for stress.

Of course, none of us knew what was going to happen. We spent those next few days in blissful innocence, doing my math and getting to know each other. I'd sit there by the hour, listening to Caulder bantering with Michael over some aspect of political science. They both were politically aware and mean-witted, and when they saw things differently — which was more often than not — things could get very entertaining. Above all, Michael was a moral person. He was always interested in the *right* thing — which is not always politically correct — and in the truth. I guess, because he had been lied to, truth was very important to him.

He was always on us about what we took for granted: two parents, a family, a house, money, love, respect, education, art. I tried to tell him it wasn't like he'd been totally deprived himself. And then he'd smile at me and tell me, well, that was right. He wouldn't fight with me. And there was not another moment in those days when Michael and I were alone together.

Every day, we expected the doctor to tell us that Michael was going home. Every day, he seemed happier and stronger, and the shadows behind his eyes didn't seem so deep.

The day before Thanksgiving, we didn't check in with the doctor. We were running a little late, and Caulder had a Big Date with Hally he had to be home for. It was one of those drive-into-the-city-have-dinner-in-a-real-restaurant things, and Caulder was nervous about it. I wasn't real happy about cutting the visit short, but Caulder had the car, so what could I do?

Actually, I think I heard the monitor before we even got to Michael's door, but I didn't think a thing about it. It never crossed my mind that I'd find it hooked up to Michael again.

Caulder stopped dead in the doorway of that room, his mouth open. "What *happened?*" he asked, before he could catch himself.

Michael was flat on his back in the bed, with the IV bottle hanging up over his shoulder, and it was like somebody had erased the last couple of weeks. He turned his head when we came in and held up one hand. He looked very groggy.

Caulder dropped all his books on the table and went straight to the bedside. I took off my coat, watching. Michael made a sleepy smile for Caulder.

"My *gosh,*" Caulder said, glancing up at the IV.

"I didn't expect you," Michael said. His voice was all muzzy and he blinked very slowly. "Doctor was going to call you." He sighed. "I guess she didn't."

194

"I'm sorry," Caulder said, putting a hand on the bed. "You can tell me not to ask, but I can't —"

Michael lifted his hand again. " 's all right," he said. "I'm all right." He closed his eyes. "It's been a long work. I'm just tired. Just finally too tired." He made another smile for Caulder. "I can't do anything with you today," he said. "Go home."

Caulder glanced back over his shoulder at me. He looked sick.

"I can't," he said.

"Listen to me," Michael said. And then he patted Caulder's hand. Caulder looked down at that hand with something like shock. I don't believe Michael had ever touched him before. "I'll be all right," Michael said, talking through a dream. "But you've got to go home. I can't do what I need to do with you here."

Caulder glanced up at the clock.

"Don't lie to me," he said. "Smitty, I couldn't stand it."

Michael let go of his hand. "I won't lie," he whispered. And he closed his eyes.

Caulder came back to where I was standing. "I can't leave him like this," he said. "I don't know what to do."

"I'll stay," I said. "You go on. I've got a lot of reading I've got to do for Monday. I'll just sit here out of the way, and I'll call my mom to come get me. No reason for both of us to stay."

He looked back at Michael. Michael hadn't moved. Caulder gritted his teeth.

"Go on," I said. "He won't even know I'm here."

Caulder looked up at the clock again and then checked his watch. "Okay," he said. "But if you find

195

anything out, you call me." He picked up his books and sidled out the door.

I followed him out into the hall. "I'll call you," I promised, whispering. He waved and went slowly off down the corridor. I went back into Michael's room and sat down. It was very quiet. The monitor blipped softly away in the corner, and the wind blew outside the window.

"Why didn't you go with him?" Michael asked. He hadn't opened his eyes. It only surprised me a little that he'd known I was there.

"I just thought I'd stay for a while," I said. "I won't bother you."

He did something between a laugh and a sigh. "You already have," he said. "Why are you sitting all the way over there?" His voice didn't sound quite so muzzy anymore. I got up and pulled my chair closer. "Don't you have anywhere to go?" he asked.

"Nope," I said.

"That's nice," he murmured. "Why don't you go home and get ready?"

"Michael," I said, beginning to feel a little hurt.

"I thought you had a date," he said. "Wasn't tonight the big night?"

"It was," I said.

"You didn't check in with me." The voice rang loud in the room, making me jump. It was the doctor in the doorway.

"I'm sorry," I said.

"I would have told you it wasn't a good day for you to be here." The look she gave me was pure adult reproof.

"I can't do this," Michael said to her, all muzziness vanished from his voice. He was angry.

She straightened her back and then leaned against the door frame, looking at him.

"I think you can," she said, quietly.

"*You* think I can," he said.

"Smitty — " she said.

"My name is Michael," he said, a temper I didn't even know he had lancing through the words. "Read the admittance forms." The anger on his face was as clear as anything I had ever seen there.

The doctor remembered I was there. She looked at Michael, and then she looked at me, and opened her mouth to speak to me.

"No." Michael said, abruptly. The doctor shut her mouth. A look passed between them. He disengaged. "I'll tell her," he said softly.

She folded her arms.

I wondered then if he'd finally lost the ability to hide himself behind his face, he was so obviously upset. His eyes had gone dark, seemingly focused at some point between the bed and the ceiling, his energy all turned inward. Whatever it was that was going on, it was scaring the heck out of me.

"My brother," he said at last, "is coming to visit me tonight."

I looked at the doctor. She met my eyes, but didn't say anything.

"They didn't tell me till this morning," he went on, his voice very controlled. "They were afraid of this — " he held up the arm with the needle in it. "It evidently never occurred to them that they might give me time to prepare. It never occurred to them that I might not" — something seemed to slip — "be *ready* for this." He turned those tormented eyes on the doctor. "What made you think you had the right?"

"Actually," she said, levelly, "when it comes to rights, I have your parents' consent to do whatever I feel is necessary. But as it happens, I didn't *do* this to you, Michael. This just happened. It's just real life. I didn't tell you before this morning, because I didn't *know* before this morning. Your father jumped the gun on me, and I'm sorry about that. But that's the way it happened, and now you're going to have to deal with it. Better that it happen here and now than some other time in a worse place. You can't hide from him forever, Michael. And you can't hide from yourself. You just have to deal with it. And I believe you can."

He turned his face away from her.

"Well, you're going to have to," she said again. She pushed away from the door. "You want me to goose up that drip a little?"

"No," he said, biting off the word. "I'm going to have to *deal* with it."

"Fine," she said. "I'll be in to check on you later." She turned on her heel, and she left the room.

Whatever had been holding him up through that suddenly left him. He closed his eyes and pressed his head back into the pillow. "Don't ask me," he said, abruptly.

I huddled quietly on the chair.

"I can't talk to you about my brother," Michael said, after a moment. His voice had gone very ragged.

"I didn't ask," I said, quickly.

"I know you didn't," he said. He tucked his hands

up under his armpits and shivered. "I can't go for-ward," he whispered, "and sure as hell can't go back." He lay there for another little time, and I still sat beside him, not touching him, but feeling the ebb and pull of his work. "I'm trying to tell you," he said, finally, quietly. "I *can't* . . . talk about him."

The hem of his pillow slip was coming out. The thread hung down from the bed, and I began to tug at it absently. Then I saw I was pulling the stitches out. I didn't know what to do with it after that.

"I know," he said, "he's not supposed to be able to hurt me anymore. At least, not in a lighted room, with witnesses present. I know that."

I had tucked the little thread back behind the edge of the hem, all the time trying to think clearly. I had my forehead pressed against the bars of the bed.

"He's my brother, Ginny," he said, that silent pulse in his voice, that invisible tearing. "I can't work up the hate inside to make me safe from him."

I was thinking there should be something I could do, something I could say that could defuse this. That could make him see he was strong enough to handle it. Something that could make love seem safer than hate. If you're God, you can heal; if you're not, what do you do?

"I am *so* cold," he said. But that was nice, because that, I could do something about.

"Move over," I told him.

"What?" He looked at me, surprised.

"Shove over," I said. So he did, and I climbed up next to him and curled up, my back against his

199

side. For the next few minutes, his body felt about as hospitable as a brick bed, which was no big surprise. But after a while, he began to relax against me just a little, and then a little more, until we were just there together. It was not comfortable, but it was companionable.

And then he said, softly, "Talk to me, Ginny. Tell me about your family." I felt him lay his cheek against the top of my head. "Talk about Paul and Charlie, and the other one. Make me see the difference between yours and mine. Make me angry. Make me safe. Talk to me."

That, also, I could do.

CHAPTER SEVENTEEN

"You seem to be holding your own," the doctor said, dryly. She was standing in the doorway. We'd been lying there like that for quite a while, so when I sat up, I was a little dizzy. I sat on the edge of the bed, still in contact with Michael; he stirred against my back.

"He should be here in another half hour or so," she said. Michael flinched. "We're waiting for him in my office, then we'll all come down here together. He's only a human being, Michael."

Michael was silent.

"Okay?" she asked.

She still got no answer.

"I know everything about him," she reminded him. "You told me everything. And you're okay."

"You were giving me drugs," Michael said.

"You want them now?" she asked.

"Yes," he said.

"You want me to arrange for that?" she asked.

There was a silence. "No," he said.

"Good." She looked at me. "Isn't it about time for you to go home?"

"You want me to?" I asked Michael, the cowardly half of me hoping he'd make me go.

"This is not going to be easy," the doctor said.

"And it's really none of her business."

"You can stay," Michael said to me.

I found the other half of me willing. "Your mother won't like it," I told him.

He said, "My mother's in charge of her own hell. I'm in charge of mine."

"Good," the doctor said. "An hour and a half, and this will be over." Great. It only took seventeen seconds for an earthquake to flatten San Francisco.

"I'll see you in a few minutes." She left. Michael shifted himself on the bed. I slid down and walked around to the window. It was dark outside. It got dark early, now.

I was watching a tiny figure move back and forth across a lighted window in the building over the way, and thinking I had just put myself in the middle of a very scary situation. Among the other things that bother me, I really dislike confrontations.

"Thank you for staying," Michael said. He didn't sound grateful. "But it would have been better if you hadn't come in here today."

"Why?" I asked him. "You afraid I'll lose respect for you because you're scared? You're not the only one." It was kind of early to be so dark. Storm clouds, maybe. "I don't know — maybe you're right. Maybe I will. I told you, I'm not a very responsible person."

"Commitment," he said.

"That's right," I said. "I want to go home. There's nothing scary going on there — "

"So, go."

" — but you're here," I finished. "So I'm staying." I leaned back against the wall, my hands tucked in

202

behind me. "There's something I want to know," I said. Someone was walking down the hall outside, a lady with a little boy. "Why did you let your brother do this to you?"

"Let him?" Michael asked.

"Yeah," I said. "These last four or five years. Why didn't you just — decide to stop it. You could have. Couldn't you?"

He made no answer.

"I don't know, but I've thought about this a lot, and it seems to me that after a point, you're as responsible for this as your parents are. I know I don't understand the situation. But you're a smart person, Michael. And your body isn't weak. You should have told him to kiss off a long time ago. Russell isn't God."

"You're right," he said. "You don't understand."

"Excuse me." A young, cheerful-faced guy was leaning in at the doorway. I knew him. I knew the face. But I couldn't think what class I had with him. It was a nightmare time for somebody to suddenly think of dropping in.

"Do you know where room one-ten is?" he asked. He pushed a lock of hair out of his eyes. He was really good-looking.

"This is one-ten," I answered, still trying to figure it out. I didn't even feel the ground begin to shake.

He looked at the bed. "Sure it is," he said. "How ya doin', Schmitt, old man?" And he came on into the room. He was wearing jeans and a light-blue tailored shirt and a Woodlands letter jacket. Michael had gone dead white.

"I came as soon as I heard," the young man said. Russell said. Obviously, it was Russell. Obvious when you looked at Michael's Smitty face. "Gone off the deep end, finally, huh?" That's why I knew him. I'd seen him often enough in that portrait they had hanging in the dining room. He looked over at me. "You must be a friend of his?"

I nodded. This had taken me totally by surprise.

He smiled at me, an open, very easy smile. "Then that makes two of us," he said, and he leaned across the bed and put his hand out for me. This could not be the monster, Russell. I shook his hand before I knew what I was doing. Now I realized — I'd thought he was good-looking because he looked so much like Michael. "I'm Russell," he said.

"Virginia," I answered, realizing only later that I'd given him my distance name. The doctor had warned us in the beginning; all the Russell stories, all that information, had been based on Smitty's perceptions of reality. Smitty's maybe-not-so-objective perceptions. This person was not the person I had expected.

"I didn't know Smitty had such pretty friends," Russell said. He looked down at Michael and patted his knee, affectionately. "It's been a long time since I've seen my old buddy here. Long time. Too bad about this." He looked around the room. "It could be worse though, couldn't it?"

Michael's breathing had gone pinched. He definitely wasn't as good as he used to be at setting his face in stone.

"Well," Russell said. "I'm glad you're here. I've always wanted the best for you. It's time you let somebody take care of you."

"I should go tell them you're here," I said.

He smiled at me. "Sure," he said. But I didn't go. I didn't like to leave Michael.

Russell leaned over and he picked up Michael's hand. "I just thought I'd pop in here before the family stuff starts. I just wanted to tell you, I've got a job offer. They tell you that? A good one. My little Christine, she's excited about that. It's real important to me. It'll take me out of state, and I'll probably never see you again, old Schmitt, sad as that seems. Be outta your hair."

It was only then that I saw what he was doing to Michael's hand. It was the odd angle that caught my eye, and when I looked closer, I could see the white marks around the places where Russell's fingers were pressed. When I saw it, I knew he'd taken me for a ride, just like he'd done everybody else, all these years. I felt like I'd betrayed my friend in those few moments, and now a terrible rage washed through me.

"Don't," I nearly shouted, and before I knew what I was doing, I'd moved forward, threatening.

Russell looked up at me, innocent surprise on his face. He released Michael's hand, looking oh-so-reasonable and kind of hurt. But now I could see right through it. "I'm sorry," he said, as though he couldn't understand why I had taken offense. "I just thought he'd want to get caught up." He patted Michael's hand briefly. "Don't forget," he said. "I love you, Smitty-boy. I'd hate to see you get hurt." He gave me an ironic little wave, and left the room.

I collapsed back against the wall. I was flushed hot with guilt. I hadn't even heard the monitors screaming at me. I pushed away from the wall and

205

leaned over Michael, who was lying there as if he were dead.

"That is *exactly* what I mean," I hissed. "Why did you let him do that? Why didn't you just *rip* your hand away from him. *Look* at you. Why don't you just *hit* him? *I* would. Before I let anybody do this to me, I'd hit them with a *chair*."

His jaw was set. I was angry at him because I'd just stood there and let it happen. "You're worth more than this," I told him. "You're a hundred times the human being he is. And you're not helping him out any, letting him *think* he's God." I clamped my teeth shut and pushed air out through them.

Michael was breathing hard, but he didn't say a thing.

I went back around the bed and dropped into my chair. My hands were shaking like crazy, but now I was mad. And a little surprised at myself. I felt very fierce, and I wasn't used to that. I kind of liked it, actually. I certainly wasn't nervous anymore. And I was almost eager to get them in here and get this whole stupid thing over with.

Those last few minutes took a very long time, and Michael didn't say another word until we heard the voices down the hall. But then he said to me, "Don't leave." Like he really thought I would. I took hold of the bars of his bed, knowing the hardest thing coming up for me was going to be keeping my mouth shut.

"He'll do it with them, too," Michael said then, all in a desperate rush. "You saw. You believed him — they will, too. They're not going to see through it. When he's finished in here, I'm dead." He shut his eyes and put his hand over them.

"Not if you don't let it happen," I whispered as they came in. "You don't have to let him win."

They came through the door in a line, the doctor first. She came over to the bed. "Let's get you up here where you can participate," she said, and she ran the head of the bed up so that Michael was more or less sitting. He had two bright, flushed spots in the middle of his cheeks. He definitely looked vulnerable, sitting there in that bed.

Michael's parents were sort of milling around, trying to settle on what, exactly, they wanted to do. His mother caught sight of me and flicked a put-out sort of look at the doctor, then she came over to the bedside and patted Michael's hand. He didn't move. Mr. Tibbs had picked up a chair and was trying to figure out where to put it. Russell was standing in the doorway, watching it all. "We need more chairs," he said.

"The next room down is empty," the doctor said.

It was all so casual and normal.

Russell went down the hall and got the chairs. The doctor took hers and set it down by the window, out of the way. From there, she could watch them all and keep an eye on Michael and his monitor.

Russell ended up sitting with his back to the far wall, facing the bed and the two chairs his father had set up in the middle of the room. Michael's parents were half turned away from the bed, facing Russell. They all sat down and arranged themselves, and a silence settled in the room. Michael closed his eyes.

"Michael. Your family wants to start," the doctor said.

"*Michael*, is it, now?" Russell said.

"Not really," his mother said, looking around at the doctor. I was looking at the doctor now, too. Michael's eyes had come open.

"Well, he's a big boy, now," Russell said. "He has a right to a real name." He cocked his head and launched himself out of the chair and across the room toward the bed. "I haven't said 'hi' to you yet, *Michael*. Hey, Mom. He looks pretty good. How've you been, kid?"

"Sit down, Russell," the father rumbled.

"Honey," Mrs. Tibbs said, sotto voce, "at least let him be nice to Smitty." She looked up as Russell made his way back to his chair. "Call him Smitty, darling," she said. "Let's not make this any stranger than it already is."

"Fine, Mom," Russell said, slipping into his chair. He leaned back in it, put his feet out, and crossed them. "How's Uncle Burt?" he asked.

"Oh, he's doing better," Mrs. Tibbs said. "He's — "

"Maggy," Mr. Tibbs said. She looked at him and her chin came up. Then she straightened her shoulders and dropped her eyes. "Thank you for asking, Russell," she said.

"I just wondered," he said. And then he looked up at the clock and pulled himself up straight. His parents stirred slightly in their chairs. There was not a flicker from Michael. "I guess we'd better begin," Russell said. "Though I have to tell you, I'm really not sure I understand what this is all about."

"I told you on the phone — " his father started, but Russell cut him off.

"I know what you told me. I just don't understand

the part I'm supposedly playing here. We all know that Smitty has problems. It's been obvious for years that he's got some kind of brain damage. Okay — but what I really don't understand is why — after all these years — you should suddenly feel like any of these problems could be attributed to the relationship between Smitty and me."

"Russell — " his mother started.

He held up one hand. His mother stopped. "This really hurts me, Mom." His face had this kind of hallowed sadness on it. Suffering. "This started long before I was old enough to know what was going on. How can you even think this had something to do with me?"

"Russell, we didn't — " his mother started again.

"I mean, I'm glad to be here. I'm glad to know some kind of progress is being made. But I'm going to be frank with you — I spent *years* of my life nursemaiding this kid. The whole time I was growing up — you" — he indicated both parents with a flick of his hand — "had your work, and your committees, and your clubs — "

"Please don't make it sound like I was gone all the time, Russell," Mrs. Tibbs said.

"But you were," he said.

"There were things I had to do outside of our home, yes. But I was home — "

"You were gone a lot," he stated, and he didn't wait for her to answer. "I took care of the kid for you. Half my life, I spent taking care of this kid. It just" — he looked away for a moment, his eyes glittering — "really about *kills* me that you'd come back to me now with this. This is, like, gratitude?

It just seems so trendy, mother. I'm sorry to be emotional. But this is very, *very* upsetting to me."

"Russell," his father said. "These are things that Smitty has told us himself." So polite, his parents were being with him, so respectful. *Can't you see through this? Just tell him. Take control*, I wanted to say to them.

"And isn't that tremendous?" Russell went on. "That he's finally able to communicate. I think that's wonderful. I really do. But" — he gave them a hard, righteous look — "please remember, *I* was the one who took care of him when *you* weren't home. *I* was the one who had to say 'no' to him. *I* was the one who was there, pulling him out of trouble. I mean, I think it's fairly obvious that he's going to remember me the way most kids remember their baby-sitters — most kids are going to have resentments about people who don't let them get their own way —"

Smitty's mother looked over at her husband. This was making sense to her. I'm afraid I was listening with my mouth hanging open.

"We *have* just heard one side of it," she whispered.

"I don't think we need to hear any more of Russell's side," Mr. Tibbs said.

"Just a minute," she said, her cheeks gone flush. "What do you mean, you don't need to hear it?"

"Don't you think we've heard enough?" he asked, staring at her. "After all these years, I think I've heard enough."

Her mouth dropped open. "*You've* heard enough? You've never heard *anything*. You've never listened. You *never* listen. Maybe if you had ever taken any interest in Russell from the beginning . . ."

Michael's eyes closed. There were little beads of sweat at the inside corners of his eyes.

"Mother," Russell said, sounding almost genuinely gentle. She turned from Mr. Tibbs to Russell. She subsided. She lifted her chin again and took an even breath. "So, you're saying," she said to Russell, almost as though the last few moments had never happened, "that these things your father told you about never actually happened."

"Oh, I'm sure, in Smitty's mind, that was just the way it seemed. Who knows how he thinks? But no. Of course not." He swept his face to the side, his eyes glistening again.

"The doctor doesn't seem to think it's quite that simple," Mr. Tibbs began.

"Well," Russell said, an ironic twist at one corner of his mouth. He shifted in his chair and spoke with his head slightly to the side, as though he were speaking only for his parents. "Exactly how much is all this setting you back, Dad?"

Dr. Woodhouse and I made eye contact. Mr. Tibbs's face was growing darker by the minute. *Good,* I thought. I wanted to stand up and scream at them — *Stop arguing with him. Stop trying to reason with him. You don't have to convince him to see the truth — he knows the truth. Russell is the truth.*

"I mean," Russell said, throwing himself back in the chair with both hands lifted, "not that being here isn't probably doing him some good . . ."

"Your mother and I," Mr. Tibbs said, and now it seemed like he was holding himself in, "would like you to stay here for a while and work with your brother, and see if we can get this thing straightened around."

211

Russell's face took on a very intent, thoughtful look. "Well," he said, "I know you'd *like* me to do that. And I think it's important. And I did a lot of running around, yesterday, to see if I could arrange it. But" — he spread his hands — "you have to remember — I'm in the middle of a semester. There was nothing I could do. I've got to finish it. Look, it was hard enough for me to take off this weekend. They won't let me take the time out. If I leave, I'm going to lose the entire semester."

"We'd really like you to," his father said again. It was beginning to sound like a warning.

"Dad," Russell said. "I understand. But you've got to understand. I *can't*."

"I'm not asking you," his father said, finally. "I'm telling you."

"*John*," Mrs. Tibbs said, looking at her husband with wide, offended eyes.

Russell looked away, seemed to be gathering in his patience. When he spoke again, his voice had a little more edge to it. "Christy and I are getting married at Christmas. I'll have my master's by spring. I have a *very* good job offer — "

"You didn't *tell* us," his mother said. "Who made the offer?"

But Russell went right on, ". . . so it's just not possible for me to take the time out right now."

The Tibbses were looking at each other. There was definitely a struggle going on between them. Russell shifted in his chair impatiently. "Two sons," Mr. Tibbs said to her. I barely heard it. The look held between them for a minute longer. When Mrs. Tibbs finally spoke, it was without breaking that connection with her husband.

"Russell," she said, carefully. "We understand all that. But we feel this may be more important."

"More important?" He looked at her, his face unbelieving. "More important than my *life*?" Russell dropped back in his chair, his face gone a few shades paler, looking shocked — and then came outrage. "All my life, it hasn't been me who mattered. All you could ever see is *him*." There was a lot of quiet, held-in emotion in Russell's voice, now, a lot of wounded innocence mixed with some very genuine anger. I recognized the tone. I'd used it myself a time or two. "I'm not going to screw up my life now. Not because of *him*. I think I've given up enough. I'm not going to let this kid ruin the rest of my life."

"Russell — " his mother said, putting one conciliatory hand out. Russell was turning his face away from her when someone behind me spoke.

"What about my life?"

I nearly jumped.

Everyone stopped and turned and stared. The words rang in the room even though they had been said very quietly.

Michael had spoken.

The hot spots still burned high in his cheeks. His voice was throaty and low. His eyes were steady. Only the doctor, who had her eye on the monitor, and I, who could feel the rhythms of Michael's fear through the bars of the bed, knew what those words had cost him.

It stopped Russell only for a moment. And then he collected himself and gave Michael a long, cool, almost amused once-over.

"Well, he *can* talk," Russell said. "Congratulations." The parents turned slowly back to him. Russell pursed his lips, his eyes hot on Michael. "Well, I'm real sorry about your life, *Mikey*," he said. "But I don't see that that's my problem."

"How can you say that?" I asked. I knew I shouldn't have spoken, but I couldn't stand it anymore.

Russell was looking at me, now. Still surprised and amused. "There comes a time," he said, making it clear that he was choosing, for the moment, to be patient with me, "when you have to realize that you're not responsible for the whole world."

"He's your *brother*," I pointed out.

"He would have been my brother," Russell said. "If he'd been normal."

"Well, we believe he may be normal. At least — " Mrs. Tibbs began.

"He's not," Russell cut in. "Look at him. Look where we are."

"I'm not normal," Michael said, still quietly, his eyes on Russell's. "But I'm not a liar." The monitors were all at peak, and the doctor was sitting slightly forward.

Russell gave him a long look. "Well, neither am I," he said.

"You've got to be kidding," I said.

"Excuse me," he said, turning that look on me. "Who is this *girl*, Mother? Is she part of our family?"

"Well, actually — " Mrs. Tibbs started, turning around to me, definitely annoyed.

"She has a right to be here," Michael said. And he slipped one hand down through the bars to cover mine.

A definite leer surfaced on Russell's face. "*Really,*"

he said. "The brain-damaged kid's got a little girl-friend? That's kind of kinky."

Michael's hand had tightened on mine. If he was worried about my feelings, he shouldn't have been; there was nothing a bottom feeder like Russell could have said that would have hurt me.

Russell turned back to his parents. "I'm not staying. Do what you want with him — fine. But I'm not going to waste any more of my life playing nursemaid to this *retard*."

There was a long silence.

"There won't be any more money until after this is taken care of," his father said, quietly.

Russell drew back, slowly. "You've got to be kidding," he said.

Michael said, softly. "Did you tell your Christy why you were coming here, Russ? Or maybe you intend for her to take my place."

Russell came up out of his chair violently, his eyes burning and his fists clenched — but then he caught himself, not even all the way up. Caught himself, and stopped and let himself back down into the chair, erasing everything that had been on his face.

Too late. Everybody'd seen it — the ugliness, the intent. And the change. If Michael had been good at emotional privacy, now we all knew where he'd learned it.

"Oh, Russell," his mother breathed.

"Well, did you hear what he said?" Russell demanded, his eyes burning holes in Smitty. "He'd drive anybody nuts. *Anybody!*" Russell looked at his mother. "You can cut off the money — you can do whatever you want. But I am not staying."

Mr. Tibbs stood up. "I've had enough," he said. "For your mother's sake, I've let this go. Years and years, I've let this go, God forgive me. But, this is the end. You have no choice, Russell. Whatever we have to do to keep you here so that we can try to undo what we've done — if we have to bring charges against you, whatever — we'll do it. This has gone on long enough. It's over."

"What are you going to tell your friends?" Russell asked his mother, his voice ugly with contempt. "Because if you keep me here, you're going to have to tell them something."

"I don't know," she said, brokenly.

"You could just let me go," he offered. "You wouldn't ever have to hear from me again — "

But his father had finally decided.

Russell turned his hatred full on Michael. "I warned you," he hissed. "Just remember that I warned you."

The doctor stood up. "If you all would please join me in my office — " Russell's eyes were still on Michael. He stood up slowly and it crossed my mind that he might actually try to do something, right here in front of everybody — but all he did was leave the room. And when he left, the darkness went with him.

Mrs. Tibbs followed her son, but her husband lingered behind. He didn't come near the bed, but stood awkwardly facing it. "I just want you to know," he said, not quite looking at his son. "We're sorry. I can't tell you how sorry."

His words had faded into silence when Michael finally answered him. "Thank you," was all he said.

His father nodded, as though that answer was more than he had expected, and then he turned and followed his wife.

The doctor was looking down at Michael. "The hard thing now will be coming to the point where you can forgive. They'll need that from you. Your parents. Almost as much as you need it yourself." She didn't wait for him to answer; she knew he wouldn't. She nodded at me and she, too, left the room.

It was very quiet after that.

No stirring in that room except the sound of our breathing and the soft rhythm of the monitor.

And then I began to realize, I felt like I'd been completely emptied.

I was feeling *great*.

I felt like I could do anything, like I could handle anything. Like every particle of fear had just been burned right out of my soul.

Michael was just lying there looking up at the ceiling. And then suddenly, he was hit with this terrific full-body shudder. He looked a little surprised as he went through another tremor, and another one after that. He looked at me, helplessly, shivering hard.

"So, now I'm falling apart?" he asked, teeth almost chattering. He rubbed at his eye with one hand, and I could see how hard he was trembling. "My gosh," he said, hugging himself. "I thought I was cold before."

I got up and tucked the blanket around him. "Reaction," I said, almost sure I knew what I was talking about. He pursed his lips and blew, a cold weather sound, and I pulled the blanket up close under his chin. "It'll wear off," I promised. And it did, after a few minutes.

When it was over, he heaved a deep sigh, as though he were cleaning out his whole soul. After that, he was just still for a while.

He finally shook his head wonderingly, and slid both hands up over his heart.

"So, now what?" he asked, softly.

"You've got a paper due for Leviaton on Tuesday," I said.

He looked at me like he hadn't quite understood, but then a light went on behind his face, and he laughed. "I guess I do." He closed his eyes and sighed again. Then he opened one eye and squinted up at the clock. "Shouldn't you go home?" he asked.

"So, you done with me now?" I asked him.

"You have somewhere to go," he reminded me.

"No, I don't," I said.

"The big night?" he said. And then, pronouncing every word carefully, "The Big Date."

I shrugged. "I told him I couldn't go."

That evidently took him by surprise. "Why?"

"Look," I said, sidestepping. "If you want me to go home, fine. I'll call my mom. But all I'd end up doing is sitting around all night, thinking about you. If you *want* me to go out with somebody else, I could probably arrange that, too. Then I'd be with somebody else, thinking about you. If that's what you want me to do, fine. Just say so."

He glanced at me and then looked out the window.

"This was the hardest thing," he said after a minute. "And it didn't come out like I expected." He shifted on the pillow. "Russell didn't win. He didn't crucify me." He shook himself, this time a voluntary shudder, like he was shaking something off. "You know, this is the first time in my life I remember being able to *breathe*. It's over, and — it's just over."

He opened his hands. "I am amazed," he said, quietly. "I am absolutely amazed." He looked up up at the hand that had the IV attached to it. "I don't need this anymore," he said, tugging lightly at the tube. He looked at me, and there was a sudden subtle air of abandonment about him. "I'm never going to need this again. I should just rip it out."

"I don't think so," I told him.

"Maybe not," he agreed.

He peered at the dark window. "I'm really hungry. I couldn't eat anything, all day today. I want a pizza."

Suddenly, he fixed me with that look of his. "You know I don't want you to go." His voice had gone a little throaty. "I hate Zabriski."

I couldn't look at him.

"You want a pizza?" he went on happily, as if he'd never said those things. "We could order one. I could order one. But I don't think they'd deliver it here." He considered. "I don't have any money to pay for it anyway. You don't think Russell would pay for it, do you?" And then he lay back on his bed and closed his eyes and smiled.

"You're crazy," I said.

"No," he said. "No. Maybe so. But not like before."

"No," I agreed.

After a moment, he turned onto his side, facing

me. Resting his chin on the back of his hand, he considered me for a long moment. Of course, I couldn't meet his eyes. But it wasn't all that easy to look away, either. This was all making me very nervous.

"You want to come back up here?" He meant, on the bed.

"Uh-uh," I said. "Not on your life. Ever again." And whether he really meant it or not, I was getting these weird chills all over. "You're in your right mind, now," I pointed out — a pitiful stab at humor.

"Yes," he said, softly. "Maybe so. For the first time in a long, long time." He reached out as though he were going to touch my hair, but then he didn't do it. I glanced at him. He was focused inward, now. "I think," he said, "I'm beginning to understand what people mean when they talk about hope. I never expected to feel this. That there are possibilities. That I can move, now. In any direction." When he said this, there was an incredible airiness in it — he had spoken the little poem, the spirit of it, in just those few words. It left me a little light-headed, a little disoriented in time. He closed his eyes, and I could hear the softness of his breathing.

And then he opened his eyes again. There was no giddiness left in him, now. He was studying me as though he was trying to memorize my face, or read it — maybe unlock it. "What now?" he asked, his voice low, almost a whisper. The look in his eyes totally unnerved me. I started to remind him about Leviaton's paper again because that was the only thing that would come to my mind.

"With you," he insisted, holding my eyes. It

seemed to me we were breathing the same air, we were so close.

"What do you mean?" I asked, and I had to work to get the words past my throat.

He put out his hand. Not asking for mine, but as though he were trying to touch some airy verge he sensed between us. I sat back a little, trying to remember that I still had to breathe. I put a hand out, too — hesitantly, because I wasn't sure what he wanted. He focused himself on our hands, now, and he touched his fingertips to mine. And then he was looking at me again.

"The mystery," he said, softly, "is solved. Now you know everything there ever was to know. Now you can go home."

"I don't want to go home," I said, almost desperately.

His fingers slid around mine until our hands were interlocked. He closed his eyes. In a moment, eyes still shut, he asked, "Why?"

I swallowed. My eyes were burning a little bit. "Because," I said, raggedly, "I love you."

He winced, still blind. I had known he would do that. "Michael," I said, unhappily, "please. Let me stay for a while, now, and let me come back tomorrow, and another day, and another, and let me show you. I can show you. I'm not asking you to belong to me, and I'm definitely not talking about sex. I'm just talking about the way people take care of each other, the way they share life between them. I'm talking about the kind of love that keeps you alive. Please. Michael." And then a terrible thought occurred to me. "Unless there's someone else you want."

After a moment, he opened his eyes. He looked at our hands, still connected.

"Anyway," I said, blinking, because now I was crying, "you still have to help me with my math, don't you?"

He smiled. And then he let go of my hand. He touched my cheek with one finger. It came away wet. He took it all in very thoughtfully, and then he looked at me. "That's important," he agreed.

"Yes," I said. "It is."

He touched my face again. "Show me, then," he said, softly.

I guess it was kind of a reaction to the evening. Anyway, I really cried after that. And for a few minutes, I was pretty much lost inside of myself. But then, by degrees, I began to realize — Michael the solitary, Michael the emotionally crippled — Michael, my friend — was holding me.

And that called for a completely different kind of crying.

EPILOGUE

Of course, that wasn't the end of the story. I'm not sure the story will ever be completely finished. To this day, Michael hasn't really been able to forgive Russell, and it troubles him. He has gotten to the point where he can speak to his mother. And he eventually found a common interest in history with his father — albeit his dad's interest tended to be less political than automotive.

They kept Russell at the clinic for several months, testing him and working with him. I don't know what is wrong with Russell. Caulder thinks that every person comes to the hour of his birth with his personality already in place, for good or bad — and that his life afterward will shape what is already there.

I think that things happen, and that, if we don't do something to change them, they just keep happening. Sometimes that's a good thing, and sometimes it's a nightmare.

And it's been very hard for Michael. They kept him in the hospital till nearly Christmas. It seemed interminable to all of us, but it was only the beginning of a long process. You don't undo years of behavior in a couple of months. But he does have a strong mind and a strong body, and those things, together with his luck, have helped him turn his anger and his intense hunger for human meaning into something closer to compassion than to despair.

He has made a solemn promise to himself that there will be no cycling of his trauma — that whatever he finds of Russell in himself, whatever cruel or unhappy or dishonest things, he will drag them out into the light and deal with them. I've never heard him tell a lie, nor have I heard him say a damaging word to anybody. Not ever. It's joy and light he wants; he has been on the other side of darkness, and he doesn't intend to go back.

Anyway, once he finally came home, they decided not to send him back to school. It was our last year, and he was so far ahead, anyway; it wasn't like he was going to miss anything but the stress.

But his mother was concerned that he'd lose too much if he just sat around for all those months until college. So she took Caulder's mom's advice, and "sent" Michael to study with my mother, the local educational hobbyist.

And that's how it happened that Michael got worked into the fabric of our family, and how Michael and Charlie — and, eventually, Paul — became so close. And that is how Michael gradually became a permanent fixture in my life.

On one of the typical million, million nights of his new life, Michael ate dinner with us, and Caulder came over after. We all sprawled around the fireplace — Caulder lost somewhere in his dreams, Michael and Charlie playing cards, James generally messing around, and my folks reading the paper.

"Ginny got an application from a school in California today," Charlie said. "Give me three cards."

"Did you?" Michael said, looking over at me.

I nodded.

"Is it a good school?" he asked.

I shrugged.

"You going there?" Charlie asked.

"I haven't decided," I said.

"They haven't accepted you," James pointed out.

"James," Mother said, wearily. "Why don't you put your exuberance out for the night and go get a book to read? *Now?*"

"You got any acceptances?" Charlie asked Michael.

"It's kind of early for that, isn't it?" Mother asked.

"I have some," Michael said. "My mother had the applications out last year."

Charlie had to work to get Michael to tell him which schools he'd heard from. It turned out there were some impressive names on the list. Not a surprise.

"They going to fight over you?" Charlie asked.

Michael looked up, surprised. "I hope not," he said.

"So, have you decided?" Charlie put his cards down.

"Have *you?*" Michael countered, and laid his cards down carefully in front of my brother.

Charlie hissed and sat back. "I shouldn't have taught you this game. Juilliard."

"You never told *me* that," Mother said.

"What?" Dad asked.

"He's decided to go to Juilliard," she said.

"Who?" Dad asked.

"Who do you think?" Mom said, giving him a funny, fond look. "*Charlie.*"

"Really," Dad said, looking thoughtfully at Charlie.

"So," Charlie went on, not to be put off. "What about you?" He dealt another hand to Michael.

"I don't know," Michael said. He was not talking about it.

"They still going to take you, even though you don't finish out this year?" Charlie asked.

"They've already accepted me," Michael reminded him. He started rearranging the cards in his hand.

"So," Caulder said from his stomach on the hearth rug, cheek on his hands, "Why haven't you decided?"

"I don't know," Michael said. "Two cards."

"You just choose the best one," James said.

Michael glanced at him. "That makes sense," he said.

"You worried about cutting it in the Ivy League?" Caulder asked him.

Michael looked at him. "Aren't you?"

"Man," Caulder said, "don't worry about that. You've been top honors all your miserable life."

Michael did his funny little smile, and then he pulled out another two cards. "What else did I have to do?" he asked, and he put the cards down. "Two."

"I already gave you two," Charlie said.

"I'm going to Georgia Tech," James said. He'd taken a place in the corner, by the fire, and he had a book propped up against his knees. "No. Cal Tech. Cal Tech."

"That's going to take some work," my mother

said, shooting a little look at my dad.

"What are we going to do tonight?" I asked, stretching.

"Just exactly what we're doing," Caulder said dreamily.

I slapped him lightly on the back. "I thought you were supposed to be going out with Hally," I said.

"I am," he said. "Later."

"Do you want company?" Michael asked, not looking up from his cards.

"Got you now," Charlie chortled. He put his cards down again.

Michael put his down, too, looking apologetic. And Charlie fell over backward onto the couch.

Caulder got this wicked grin on his face. "Not really," he said. I poked Caulder in the ribs. He rolled away onto his side and scowled at me. "Sure he does," I said. "He just loves it when we all tag along."

"I'm sure he does," Michael said.

"We could go to the Film Society," James said. "Are the girls coming over?"

"Later," Caulder grunted, rolling back onto his stomach.

"What's the movie?" Charlie asked.

I went to check the schedule. "*The Philadelphia Story*," I told them.

My mom looked up. "Oh, you'll *love* that." We all looked at her. "No, really — you will."

"It's one of her favorites," I said, serenely.

"Jimmy Stewart," my mother said, retiring behind her paper with dignity. "Katharine Hepburn. Cary Grant."

"Let's do it," Caulder said.

"Anything traumatic in it?" Michael asked.

"Nothing worth walking home over," I said, grinning at him.

"That's very funny," he said.

"Witty," my mother went on from behind the paper. "Urbane. *Killingly* romantic."

"Ah," Michael said again. This time with more interest.

"Hally and I'll sit in the back so we can smooch," Caulder said.

"That's where Charlie and I love to sit," James said, cheerfully. "In the back."

"Romantic, huh?" Charlie said. He picked up the cards and handed them to Michael.

And Michael was giving me this look from across the room that brought heat up in my cheeks, and embarrassed me, and made me turn around to check if my mother had seen.

"What are *you* grinning at?" James asked me.

"Shut up," I said.

"So, okay," Caulder said. "I'll go call Hally." He got up on his knees and looked around at all of us. "Decided?"

"Decided," James said, from the corner.

"You won't be sorry," my mother said.

"Decided," Michael said.

And he put the cards down.

KRISTEN DOWNEY RANDLE

is the author of several novels, though *The Only Alien on the Planet* is her first for Scholastic Hardcover. She lives in a glade on the banks of the Provo River with a bearded husband, four sturdy, if fanciful, children, and a blue merle collie who only *appears* to be crosseyed.

Ms. Randle spends her time reading, quilting, teaching algebra, and keeping a watchful eye over the moral and financial deportment of the dozen or so musicians who frequent the family recording studio. She believes very much in the power of the human soul for making things right.